CU00925483

A CATALOGUE FOR THE END OF HUMANITY

Timothy Hickson

'A Catalogue for the End of Humanity'
An anthology of published and original fiction

by Timothy Hickson

Cover illustration by Raja Nandepu —
raja.artstation.com
Edited by BK Bass

Additional illustrations by:
Alice in Foxland
Agnieszka Świerkot
Ellie Gordon
Kristina Petrova
Feier Shen
Tyrone Le Roux
Yovina K. Tandiharja
Markus Yu

First paperback edition published in 2023.
ISBN: 978-1-7386224-0-5

For Laura

CONTENTS

Foreword

The joy of short fiction is like trying on a flashy new outfit, giving it a twirl in the mirror, and seeing how it looks on you. You might briefly slip into Bora Chung's deeply uncomfortable body horror in 'The Head', or perhaps Hilma Wolitzer's grounded and intimate writing in *Today a Woman Went Mad in the Supermarket*. One page you're reading Ted Chiang's meditative and touching 'Story of Your Life', and the next you're getting an insight into the American psyche around the Vietnam War with *The Things They Carried*. If you're not enjoying it, it'll be over soon. If you are, you're left wanting more. I can only hope this book leaves you wanting more.

This collection is an eclectic mix in many ways. Some stories are snapshots of daily life, of struggles with faith, mental health, and identity. Others have artificial intelligence, distant colonies, and aliens from eons past revealing themselves. I realized some time ago my writing often deals in death and endings. Five of the stories in this book even allude to or explicitly mention death in their titles, while others discuss it in their own way. Am I a pessimist? I don't think so, though my wife might disagree, and she usually has a better grasp of me than I do. I also tend to write about where to find hope when faced with the end, be it of the universe, of life, of us, or of a relationship—which sometimes *is* the world.

I tend to use fiction to process my thoughts, untangle complex questions, and pin them down to some shadow of an answer. I know this opens me up to endless speculation, but my fiction is just as much for me as it is you. I read in the same way.

These days, we have our pick of apocalypses. We're not running short of them. Sometimes, it can feel like humanity isn't worth it. And yes, one day, some unknown years from now, the last human will take their last breath and set their eyes on one final sunset, but when that day comes, I choose to believe it will be a sad one. I suppose this collection is just as much about how terrible we can be as well as how miraculous we are. I spend a lot of time writing as I try to make sense of it, navigating these questions. I know I'll never arrive at a final answer, as if there is one, but hopefully I find better questions to ask— a new normal with a little more hope and direction. With this in mind, *A Catalogue for the End of Humanity* seemed like an extremely apt title—a catalogue you peruse to see what's on offer.

In my younger and more vulnerable years, I thought I just didn't *like* short fiction. It wasn't for me. I distinctly remember writing an essay on Shirley Jackson's 'The Lottery' in school, as well as doing exams with unfamiliar texts, but when I sat down to write, I dreamt up 'big' stories that stretched for hundreds of pages. I couldn't contain myself. Short fiction felt unambitious. I was wrong, of course. They may be short, but nothing about these stories is 'little'—though I wouldn't be the first child to emerge from the national curriculum with a warped perception of just how incredible short stories can be. When I finally threw myself into reading them again, I never looked back.

I fell in love with Ted Chiang first, but even more so, I loved flitting from genre to genre, author to author, and style to style. One moment with Aimee Bender's contemporary magical realism and the next with Choi Eun-young's South Korean perspective. It was inspiring. The more I read, the more I wanted to read.

Short fiction hasn't just transformed my reading tastes but my writing too. It's easy to get stuck in one style, especially when we're working with the same story, the same characters, and the same themes. Short fiction lets you try on all these different styles to see what fits best, what doesn't, and learn. You can experiment quickly, almost frivolously. It can be hard to judge your own work when sticking with a single novel for what might be years at a time. I know I struggle with that. Short fiction has given me confidence in my work, not only because I could quickly compare one story to another and see where I improved, trying new things every time, but because I could send my work out for publication.

I began publishing short fiction some years ago now (and some stories in this collection are noted for where they were originally published). 'Two Robots at the End of the World' almost landed in *Clarkesworld* before it was picked up by *Utopia*. Publication helped me see where my strengths were—as well as my weaknesses— but more importantly than that, it gave me a confidence in my skills I had lacked for some time. One of the stranger effects of working in the online world is how it warps your perception of yourself and your work. Not only are you constantly under a barrage of comments from others reviewing you, but there's often little correlation between the work you put in and the success of any given thing you create. Short fiction was an escape from all that. Not to say the publishing world is much better, but it was just me and my work—no audience, no comments, no analytics. I had a better measure of myself. Sharing my writing with magazines and friends was a blessing, and *A Catalogue for the End of Humanity* grew out of that. It is more 'me' than anything I've put online.

If this is your first real shot at short fiction, then it's my privilege to be part of that. If it's not, then it's still my privilege. I want to thank Laura, my wife, who has always forced me to see the bright side and who is the strongest and clearest example of humanity being miraculous. I also want to thank Ellie, whose eagerness to read my work makes all the difference in the world, and whose feedback is invaluable.

Stay nerdy,

Tim.

Two Robots at the End of the World

First published in *Utopia Science Fiction Magazine*
Selected for the 'Best Of' *Utopian Anthology*

The word 'iconoplast'—*the one who makes images or icons*—appeared on page two hundred and eleven of Toaster's dictionary.

From what he knew, humanity used dictionaries for moral and personal guidance: that when they did not know what to say or do, they would open the book to a random page and find wisdom in the word they landed on. Sometimes that wisdom was abstract and open to interpretation, like the time Toaster wondered whether he should go to the spinal bridge or the milky tower and its answer was 'batrachian'—*relating to toads or frogs*—but after a morning of puzzling, he figured out he was meant to go down to the river instead where the frogs used to live. Toaster had a good time counting the rocks on the bank that day—there were three thousand, four hundred and sixty-two—so of course the dictionary was right.

A human would have figured that out in an instant, but Toaster knew his mechanical mind, made from mathematics and chrome, was not so quick with that kind of thinking. Humans had the foresight to know that putting every word they had into a single book would mean that book contained all Truth that could ever be discovered because all meaning had to be found in it.

Genius, thought Toaster.

'Iconoplast' was Toaster's devotional word of the day. It invited him to contemplate more deeply the relics of human civilisation that he and Motherboard had inherited.

They had built the concrete pillars that pierced the sky, painted every picture on those huge canvasses, and marked every street corner with mysterious red and yellow signs, and they had done it with hands far nimbler than Toaster's own, which were just two forks better at stacking boxes than bricklaying and art.

Humans were the iconoplasts of Toaster's world.

Toaster's favourite symbol was a piece of art that had survived the desolation. Plastered across the side of a building in the city square near their home in the factory, humanity must have gathered before it in ritual to admire and ponder its magnificence. It featured a woman with golden hair raising her hand, and on her middle finger was a ring—*a small circular band, typically of precious metal and often set with gemstones*—that shone like starlight, glimmering, something to believe in, to aspire to. Mesmerising. Where everything else was grey, the ring's gemstone had retained its crimson hue. Below the art piece was the name 'D. Laurentis' and the phrase 'Only some things last forever.'

The ruby ring. It represented eternity, love, life, and cultivated perfection, but it had to be earned or given. Toaster only dreamed of earning a ruby ring himself and clung to the dictionary in hopes his devotion would one day lead him there.

Motherboard's cubiform shape and half-dozen arms cast a shadow of hard-angled tentacles as she rolled over a gravelly rise to join him.

'Remember to keep your solar plates open,' she reminded him.

Toaster nudged at the horizon. 'Let's go somewhere new today.'

'We cannot go too far from the factory or—'

'Humans didn't even need to return to charging ports. They could go all over because they could recharge anywhere with these things called beds—*a piece of furniture for sleep or rest*— which somehow transferred energy to their bodies. Technology we could only dream of. I've seen them, Motherboard. No wires, no batteries, no solar plates, no plugs. Their minds must have been such incredible things to make something like that.' If Toaster's shoulders could have dropped, they would have. 'I want to see *more.*'

'The humans gave us hundreds of blocks to explore. If they knew it was good for us to go out further, then they would have designed us for it.'

'Maybe.'

'I made a picture,' said Motherboard, showing him a piece of paper scrawled with warm colours. 'It is the sunrise.'

'I like it.'

'Come on.'

The two set out to fix things and see what treasures they could find; that was what they did every day; that was *all* they could do every day. Pretty stones, tatters of flags from republics long faded, shards of coloured glass they could string together the way humans did with little lights. Motherboard had a screw function while Toaster could thread, and it made the factory a little more homely.

Humans loved putting up lights on walls, so much in fact that they did it every year *and then* took them down just so they could put them up again the next year. So, Toaster decided he loved doing that too. Just like they also enjoyed stabbing pumpkins every October and eating rabbit eggs every April.

He didn't quite understand the appeal, if he were honest, but the fallen leaves were very pretty.

Creatures of iron squatted in the wreckage of bridges and town halls, watching Toaster and Motherboard as they trekked by. Constellations of concrete and steel latched on to the morning light to make themselves more beautiful than they were, to remind themselves of what they had once looked like.

Caterpillar tracks made it easy for Toaster to traverse the rubble that had accumulated in the streets, and his suction cups made scaling walls an effortless exercise, but Motherboard had to do with rubber wheels to get around. Slower, plodding, but infinitely more careful.

Toaster tried to help her up the sheer ledges, but they were designed for different things. His chrome arms would snap under her weight if he really put his charge into it. Instead, she planted three of her six arms in a tripod arrangement on the lower level, three on the upper level, and hoisted herself up the ridge.

When it rained, Toaster needed Motherboard to shelter his dictionary inside her inner compartments, having no cupboards of his own except a small pocket sufficient only for a few wires. The dictionary still bore splotches and wrinkles from the time he was caught out under the spinal bridge in a sudden downpour. The ink inside blurred. Some of his favourite words too, like 'redintegrate'—*to make whole again.* He remembered that one, but the rest were gone forever. He would never know what they could teach him.

Toaster lamented the loss. What other wisdom had he stupidly let get washed away?

A fork appeared in their paths. Left rose over the mound of a collapsed building and right leaned into a river. The city's bones were concrete, but its veins were water, wind, and sunlight. They had taken the rightward path exactly one hundred and twelve times over the past seventy-two years and left exactly zero times.

Patterns they were great at, but Toaster did not want to follow a pattern anymore.

Motherboard had already started rolling down the familiar path when Toaster whipped out his dictionary.

'What's wrong?' she asked.

'We won't find anything new down there.'

Motherboard swivelled. 'Are you suggesting we go somewhere else?' she asked, as if it were the strangest idea she had ever heard.

Confident the dictionary would give him the right answer, he began flicking through the pages till he landed on the word 'urbicolous'—*dwelling in cities.* Humans lived in cities, but they also lived in buildings like the collapsed one that took them to the left. They did not live in rivers because they could not breathe water, except when they used a snorkel.

'We should go left. We will find something better that way,' Toaster announced, and when he explained his reasoning, Motherboard was convinced. She began chugging up the slope.

Up and down, around and over, they passed statues of small, headless humans. Toaster spent an hour finding each of their four pearly heads in bushes and under sheets of corrugated iron littered with holes. Motherboard tried to weld the heads back on, but most of them just cracked, leaving headless humans and bifurcated skulls.

'Well, we tried,' said Motherboard as the final *crack* echoed, and they watched the two halves tumble down the slope.

'Bon voyage,' Toaster said.

Motherboard pivoted. 'We can't fix everything. For every door we bolt up and fix, another building falls down.'

'Doesn't mean we shouldn't fix the doors.'

'No, I like fixing the doors, too.'

They admired the last grit of an old mural that featured bodies twisting into each other like a strange dance. Toaster scraped some of the ancient paint and smeared it on his grate to give himself rosy cheeks.

Motherboard patted him on the head to show she found it endearing.

A glint of metal at the bottom of the mural then caught the light as the sun shifted.

Toaster rolled forward and began picking apart the rubble that obscured whatever was beneath. Motherboard did all the heavy lifting in fact, and after a few minutes, they uncovered a metallic object, bent and speckled with rust, with a long shaft and a hole at one end, a button on the side, and a place to put his hands, if Toaster had any.

'What do you think it is?' asked Motherboard.

'I don't know.'

'I can't see anything down the hole,' she said, passing it to him.

Toaster had to grip it with both of his forks to hold it up. When he squeezed it, a cataclysmic *bang* shook the city from slumber. It bellowed, became a shout, then a growl, a whisper, and then the city's silence rushed back in like water closing around a stone dropped into a lake. Toaster was thrilled he could make such a sound. Motherboard feared it would bring the building down on them.

Friction had clearly created a lot of heat inside it because the shaft remained warm.

'What does the dictionary say the little metal thing is?' asked Motherboard.

'Good thinking!' he said and landed on the word 'trumpet'. '"A brass musical instrument with a flared bell and a bright, penetrating tone, often used in celebrations." That explains it! I don't quite know what all those words mean, but that must be what it is.'

'It was certainly a bright and penetrating sound. Humans were so very strange creatures.'

'We do not have the capacity to appreciate things the way they did. That sound was fine music to them. What do you think humans celebrated with it?'

Motherboard craned her optic monitor, as if she would find her answer in her environment.

'I have seen them in paintings of parades. Lots of parades. Parades for people dressed in uniforms. Parades for people dressed in green and brown and black, sometimes red. Parades outside the big dome buildings with big signs to tell the people inside the big dome buildings how much they love what they are parading for.'

'Do you think we could have a parade?' asked Toaster, imagining himself in a uniform.

'I think we might need more of us, Toaster.'

'How many?'

Motherboard ran the calculations. 'At least six.'

Toaster wheeled around in circles. 'What might we celebrate then?'

The sun had taken its place on the throne of the world. Motherboard looked up and took in its array. 'How about the sunrise tomorrow? I like the sunrise. There are so many pretty colours.'

'Like yellow.'

'And also red. There's always red.'

Grass squeezed through the cracks in the stony flat like the straggling wires they found in the fried machine-boxes on the side of the road. Motherboard paused at a sharp avenue the sunlight had carved out for flowers to bloom—little white ones with twenty-six petals and an egg-yolk centre. An incline carried rainwater to nourish them, the wind carried pollen, and they grew along a sliver of the road that scarcely avoided sunlight.

Motherboard adored the way they bent in the breeze, and she dug up the pockets of earth around them so she could stow them away for her window shelf behind her charging port back home.

When she turned around, Toaster was offering up a single daisy for her collection that he had plucked himself. Motherboard could not smell—she did not know what that meant—but she had a good idea of what she was meant to do. She took the daisy and brought it up to her monitor, made a wheezing sound by over-charging her fan, and then placed it delicately with her other daisies.

That one she would treasure especially.

Toaster had hoped the metal glint would turn out to be a ruby ring, but there was little hope of that. Rings were rare and special. Still, now he had a trumpet! A good day's haul, a unique addition, not just another bottle cap, chair leg, or vase. Vases made for a lovely array of odd shapes, but they were no trumpet or ruby ring.

By the time the sun had long passed its apex and lumbered down into the horizon, Motherboard and Toaster had arrived at a bright yellow line of paint.

The Boundary.

Toaster had only seen it a half-dozen times in the life his memory chip retained. It stretched from across the street, dipping into every crack, mounting every pile of rubble, and even climbing the walls. It was not a relic of the Old World, but a fixture of their new one.

They may have forgotten much over the years, but they always kept the data that the yellow line marked the perimeter seven-point-two-three kilometres out from the factory in a perfect circle. Travelling beyond risked not making it back to their charging port before their batteries ran out.

'But it won't kill us to go a *little* beyond the Boundary.'

'That was how Printing Press died!' exclaimed Motherboard.

'Printing Press went out alone. We have each other.'

'What could there be out there that you can't find inside the Boundary?'

Toaster pivoted, first to her, and then to the horizon where the sun blazed a golden circle crowned with crimson clouds. 'How can I know when I have not been outside?'

Then, Toaster started down the slope, pausing only to take one last look at the Boundary line before crossing it. It was the farthest from home he had ever been.

'Toaster!'

'You can go back to the factory if you're afraid, but I'm going.'

As seconds passed and Toaster rolled further out into the wilderness, he grew worried Motherboard would turn away and abandon him beyond the Boundary. He didn't *want* to be left alone. Toaster didn't understand a lot about how humans worked, but he understood that.

But then he heard her motors *whirling* up, chugging to speed for her to join him, trepidation rippling in her optic monitor blips. In a vain effort to make her feel better about the whole thing, he tried to wave his arms around to mimic dancing, but it didn't work.

'I can't just let you wander out here all on your own,' she explained.

'If it makes you feel any better, we'll take the low paths. No inclines, no wall-climbs, no stairs to conserve energy.'

'And no faster than four kilometres per hour,' Motherboard insisted.

Shadows were closing ranks around them, the formless armies of the night gathering.

When they reached a new city square, they were both overcome with awe.

The world beyond the Boundary was a reflection of the world within it, but shifted to the right and shaded over. The concrete monoliths followed the architectural patterns he knew, but they were not the *same* concrete monoliths. Streets arced and darted in similar formations without being the same. Different birds *chittered* in different trees, and the same wind and water pushed its way through wider veins of the city.

A ten-thousand-piece puzzle perfectly rearranged into a new picture, and to Toaster, more beautiful for being different.

Motherboard peered at a bed of flowers she had never seen before. Violet, with streaks of blue that leaned into red sticking out of the long grass. Swooping in close, she plucked one for her collection, and then cast aside a pocketful of her daisies to make room for it. 'Umstrokes,' she decided to call them, after the word that meant *on the border of things*, and because she found them outside the Boundary.

The two spent the night in the square, inspecting and fixing doors, uncovering secrets trapped beneath rubble, and admiring how the starlight turned grey into silver. They moved slowly to conserve energy, and Motherboard repeatedly checked in with Toaster to monitor his battery reserves: sixty-four percent, fifty-nine percent, fifty-five percent. Fifty-one percent was the absolute limit they could spare before heading back, and even then, they would need to take the low-route home.

'I am glad we came out here,' Motherboard admitted to Toaster, squatting in a mud pile. 'I was afraid.'

Toaster looked up at Motherboard. 'I would be afraid if you were not here with me.'

A creature of burnt orange then slinked out of the shadows on the far side of the square, sniffing its way down to a small stream, where it began to lap up the water.

'A fox!' exclaimed Toaster. '"A carnivorous mammal with a pointed muzzle and big bushy tail, known for being cunning!"'

'Should we be afraid?' asked Motherboard.

The fox peered at them, suspicious of the rumbling bulk of metal and the humming cannister beside it. They peered back.

'No, I don't think so. Not that kind of cunning.'

Finished its drink, the fox padded over to the patch of umstrokes and nosed the grass for something. Toaster and Motherboard followed at a distance, fascinated by the wiry creature's twitches and slinking. They halted each time its eyes snapped back to them, and then rolled forward as quietly as their motors would allow when it looked away. They each dialled their optic monitors back to the minimum: no twinkling lights or torches. Didn't want to scare their new friend away.

The fox was transfixed by something in the ground, but when they got within a few metres of the creature, it very suddenly knew something was wrong. Those metal things hadn't been so close before.

But it didn't flee like Toaster feared. Instead, the lanky thing wound its way over to them, nose first, one cautious step at a time, judging them with that mysterious ability to smell. Would it find them repulsive? Unnatural? The leftovers of a once-tremendous civilisation?

Toaster risked cranking his appendage fork up to meet the fox's nose, afraid sudden movements would cause it to flee. Even the wind stilled, waiting as the fox considered his offering, but then he nuzzled Toaster's fork, and Toaster saw himself in the creature's starlit eyes—a boxy thing with soft white optics. He wanted the curious creature to see itself in him in return.

Toaster wondered if the fox feared being alone in a dead world too.

A flight of birds scattered from the nearby trees and the fox evaporated into the dark behind the umstrokes. Toaster whirled after it, but that only pushed his new friend further away. Even if he wanted to chase the fox, he couldn't—not on the energy reserves he had left.

Wheeling over to bed of umstrokes, Toaster searched for what the fox had been nosing at before. That was when he spotted it.

A different shade of red, hidden under the flowers, caught his eye—dark, bloody, and capturing stray glimpses of moonlight that darted between the flowers.

A ruby ring!

Even more vivid than D. Laurentis' poster outside the factory. Plucking it from the dirt and holding it to the sky, it slid down onto one of his forks, ill-fitting for a mechanical appendage, but every part as brilliant as he imagined.

Its crystalline form wielded the starlight unlike anything else. Concrete buildings and cobbled streets swallowed the light whole into their shadows, glass let it pass through unmolested, and clouds strangled it, but the gemstone bent the light and cast it out again with human precision. Its golden band was elegant in its simple design, and Toaster felt more beautiful by simply wearing it, just as humans had.

But then Toaster let the ring slide off his fork and back into the dirt. 'I didn't earn it.' He rolled backwards, away from the ring, shutting down his light receptors to make the whole world dark so he didn't have to look at it.

'What do you mean?'

'You have to be given it or earn it.'

Motherboard considered her options, and then picked it up.

With two appendages holding Toaster's fork, and a third pinching the ruby ring, Motherboard slid the ring back onto Toaster's 'finger'. Motherboard decided that's what he should call it. It felt right.

'I hereby give you the ring myself and say you have earned it—for excellence in being.'

Toaster slowly let the light back in, focused on the ring. He raised his finger like the woman on the art piece back home. He couldn't cry or jump for joy, but he could spin on the spot in excitement till he tipped over.

While Toaster admired his new ring, Motherboard's attention turned to the soil he had found it in. Vases came from shelves, coloured glass came from pointy stone buildings, but rings came from human hands.

Wheeling a little closer, she used her several arms to clear away the dense undergrowth.

Milky white bone pierced the brittle layer of earth. A finger, followed by an arm, a spine, legs, ribcage, and pelvis all, but no skull, and the skeleton wasn't alone. A new feeling crept into her systems as she uncovered body after body—something she wasn't programmed to feel— a blackness that expanded inside her, took up processing space she did not have, warped her thoughts, and muddied her systems. She had seen ugly things before—

mud pools, lampposts, and weeds. Oh, how she hated weeds! They got everywhere and had no pretty colours. But this was ugly in a different way, like she never truly knew what the word meant before this.

The bodies were piled and twisted into each other, some embracing, heads removed, and there was only the black for Motherboard.

Humanity was so many things. Humanity was too many things.

'Motherboard,' called Toaster who had not seen what she had seen. 'We should celebrate!'

'I—' Her words stumbled on the blackness. 'I agree.'

The trumpet was in his hands, and he squeezed it just like the humans did to celebrate.

Another *bang* clashed with the night. Birds fled. Flowers tilted.

Motherboard collapsed.

A great hole had appeared in her engine grate. Diagnostics told her it was interfering with her cooling systems. A projectile had broken her internal fan and lodged itself inside her rotary board. She felt three of her arms go limp, like they weren't a part of her anymore. They dragged in the soil, and two of her wheels wouldn't function when she willed them, turning her on the spot. Everything was slowing down, like she was trying to conserve power, but it was draining out of her, anyway, out of that hole in the middle of her. And all Motherboard could think about was how her daisies needed to be potted.

'What happened?' called Toaster.

Her vision flickered, colours shifting in and out of focus. Blue disappeared entirely.

'I think the trumpet did something to me.' *Something the humans did to other humans.* They played the strangest music. 'It does not feel like I am celebrating.'

'What does it feel like?' asked Toaster, realising something was terribly wrong.

'I think,' began Motherboard, greys hardening into black, 'I think I am dying.'

'Death': *the end of life of a person or organism.* Death was not something Toaster feared. It was not something he was programmed to expect. It was not something he was programmed to understand.

But he did understand they wouldn't be able to put up the lights together each year anymore. There was no point in him threading them together if she couldn't screw them to the wall. And they wouldn't be able to fix any more doors. Toaster needed Motherboard to reach the higher hinges, and she needed him to pick up all the little bolts. In October, how was he meant to carry the pumpkins without her?

Death sounded an awful lot like loneliness—*sadness because one has no company.*

Before he came over, she swept the dirt back over the bodies.

'I can pull you to the factory,' he said, hooking his tiny chain onto her body and heaving, going nowhere except into the dirt. 'I can ask the dictionary.'

'Ontography': *the study of the essence of reality or being.* How did that help? He did not have the time to contemplate the mysteries. He needed answers.

Her batteries were draining too quickly: thirty-two percent.

'Did I do this?' He let the trumpet fall from his hooked forks and clatter on the ground. 'I did not mean to do this. I can—I can—'

Motherboard looked down at Toaster.

'You can stay here with me,' she replied. 'I would like you to stay here with me.'

'But you will be gone soon.' Toaster began picking up every scrap and stone he could in search of something that could help.

'I think I will be, yes.' Using her last working arm, she picked Toaster up and placed him gently down in front of her. 'But that cannot be helped.'

Motherboard knew she would become just another relic in that place. Standing as a testament to another time. For other passers-by to stop, look at, and ask, 'I wonder how that got there?'

'Will I be alone?' Toaster asked.

'Yes. I do not wish to go, but I do not believe we can stop this.' Eleven percent.

'Look,' urged Toaster. 'We can still celebrate the sunrise, can't we?'

Clouds had formed cracks of light in the pane of darkness. Liquid gold filtered through, warm.

'I would like that.'

Humanity told stories of angels that would pour out of the clouds to rescue lost souls, but none came. The sun still spread its wings and tore itself from the tethers of the Earth the way Motherboard wished she could, as it had every day for as long as her memory chip retained. As it would every day after she was gone.

The dawn melted away the moon, the starlight, and the blackness that had overtaken her. She was not programmed to feel peace. There was always work to be done, but that was over now. No more statues to fix. No more doors to weld. No more boxes to stack. Not by her.

A burning tide was washing over the horizon. It glittered with memory. Its many arms propped itself up on the mountaintops.

Four percent.

Toaster had seen many images of humans watching the sunrise and sunset. One of them always rested their head on the shoulder of the other. He had no head and Motherboard had no shoulder, but he wheeled himself up onto a large rock beside her. He tipped his optics screen onto her bonnet. It was growing colder.

'Remember to keep your solar plates open, Toaster,' she said, her audio chip fuzzing out on the last few words.

Clinging to the sunrise, Motherboard used what little power she had left to sear the fire and bronze display onto her optics. It was the last thing she would ever see, a sunrise that would stay with her forever. Crystallised, not bent, not refracted, but every strand captured perfectly.

Her optics dipped.

'Motherboard?' said Toaster, looking up at her, but for the first time, she didn't look back.

He let the ring slide off his finger. Didn't even care as it rolled across the ground, lost in the grass.

He was alone.

Maybe the dictionary had waited till the last moment to deliver. To give him real answers.

The word 'kelter'—*nonsense*—appeared on page two hundred and eighty-eight of his dictionary. He had no idea why it gave him that.

The Funeralists; or Hate in Five Parts

We lit a candle for every burned book, every scroll ground down by the sands of time, every love letter torn apart. They had someone to harvest their souls, another their sins, even one to mark the loss of children's teeth. Don't be so surprised we remembered the books. Aren't they more important than teeth?

The year was 631 BCE.

It was my first eulogy, with all the bright-eyed optimism and frantic rehearsing that entailed. Ashurbanipal, the last great king of the Assyrians, lay dead in a puddle of his own fluids. His library was forgotten, wasting away in the last gasps of Empire. The monolithic structure stood at the centre of Nineveh as a monument to a bygone age, and I could not resist stopping to behold it. It demanded my attention, my reverence. Everything about it was large: doors twice the size they needed to be, pillars like great arms holding up the sky, and brass braziers that must have once bathed the city in a bronze glow. And yet a mound of sand obfuscated the entrance, the pillars were crumbling, and the braziers had been left as blackened pits of dust and ash and time, one of them toppled face down on the ground. Every so often, the wind would scoop up the particulates and spread them across the city in a dark rain, right out to the sloped walls. I wiped some from my cheeks.

I knew instinctively—as we all did—how long each of the thirty thousand clay tablets, tapestries, and wax boards had before none would ever see or read them again. I could tell which epics would one day be recovered in excavations in the distant future, the way a doctor looks at a frostbitten hand and knows which fingers might be saved. This quarter of one tablet, or a third of another, but none of the last. I could tell which legal records merchants would dig up decades from then to sell off for a pittance, which tales children would stumble on in their adventures, and which incantations generals would seek out in search of ancient secrets and magicks. The library was older and wiser than any of them. I could tell which art pieces would never be seen again, their faces ground down by moving sands over the millennia. Many of them had already met their end.

I was careful not to disturb the tablets as I fluttered through the halls. I came upon a tablet in three pieces which had had been pushed over—not for any reason, likely by a soldier on their way out.

'I am sorry I am not here for you,' I said.

I gently pushed the pieces back together. I knew touching the books was forbidden, but how could I let it lie there, so broken, so discarded? Let it lie with dignity.

I drifted from room to room through cracks in walls and narrow passages. Memory had colonised the library's halls. It took root in every crack and crevasse, every gap the wind could whistle through, and every wall which had tumbled down, taking stories and records with them in heaps of words and numbers. I imagined rearranging all the little pieces and chips, even the little stones with single letters on them, and undoing entropy to reconstruct every story was once was. That was not allowed.

The stories were still there, just stretched out and scattered, decomposed. The whole place was time crystallised in stone, wax, and vellum, protected from a world where so little lasted for so long—except us. We had always been there, as long as beginnings, middles, and endings had. The architecture wanted you to feel small and insignificant, and it worked, with me being even smaller than most.

The only sound inside was that of cicada wings beating for a new season and the occasional droplet of water—a library's oldest enemy. I could already see how much the humidity would destroy. I could have plugged it, blocked it off with a bit of wet clay, but no—*this is not my role*, I told myself.

Rounding a corner, a great wall deep inside the library loomed before me. It reached into the dark, its face full of art and inscriptions, towering higher than any room that came before.

My wings flushed blue with wonder, and I must've stayed there for hours.

'You should have seen it,' I told one of my sisters sometime later. My wings were blushing no matter how much I tried to hide it, and she knew it, and I knew she knew it, but I tried to hide it, anyway. 'One of the walls had a thousand runes, each and every one painstakingly carved out over years, and when they have so few! To spend all that time inscribing it with such care. None of them were carved mistakenly or frivolously. They planned them all out beforehand and knew exactly where the story was going to start and end, precisely how much space it would take up on the wall, right down to the last glyph. It was beautiful, oh so beautiful, I was almost crying. Almost. I said I wouldn't cry on the job. I promised you, and I didn't, I swear, wings and all. I tried to get in, to say my piece for the tablet, and leave, just like you said, but I couldn't help but stop just... to look.'

'Everyone looks on their first day out,' she said, her own wings siphoning colour from the world around her. 'And every day you go out to a new book, a new eulogy, you'll always hope to experience that first glimpse of wonder again.'

'And it will never be quite the same?'

'I didn't say that,' she said with a smile, but I could feel something behind it she wasn't telling me. 'But it will be different.'

I didn't ask how it would be different because I didn't really want to know. I wanted to remain infatuated and awestruck, happy enough to bask in the wonders of the library and save any monotony for when it hunted me down.

Many of the library's deepest rooms were already buried under sand and rubble, their stories with them, and the one text I was there for was soon to follow. It was my job to eulogise for it and lay it to its final rest, knowing its job was finished and none would ever read it again.

'There you are,' I said.

My tablet lay in the corner, discarded underneath a collapsed shelf and beneath an unstable roof whose pillars were on the verge of crumbling. I touched the ground so lightly I left no footsteps in the sand. I folded my wings behind my back and raised a hand to the tablet like you might cup a lover's face, feeling every crack and groove time had inflicted upon it. It looked so sad, so ready to be taken. In two decades, the roof would collapse, and the tablet would fragment into a dozen tiny pieces. The tumult of the sand would grind the cuneiform runes from its face and its story would be forgotten forever. It would simply fade from peoples' minds. Later excavations would rescue only a tiny portion of the thousands of tablets, and this was not one of the lucky ones.

I lit my candle by pinching the wick between two fingers. I jumped back in reflex as the little flame illuminated the surrounding library, shadows catching on every edge. My fingertips were left with two warm ash marks. The candle still had its new and perfect shape back then. It would seem wrong to my eye now. Candles come into existence as drooping, haggard things with streaks of wax down one side or the other. But I remember, so vividly, watching that first pool of white wax melt till a breach formed in the side and a single droplet ran amok, down to gather at the base where it once again formed into hard wax.[1]

---

[1] It is unclear whether this ritual reflects some other, older ritual from the Before, either wholly or in part, or whether this ritual was in fact practised by the Funeralist's contemporaries. While some

The candle's flame elucidated chapters, colophons, and rhymes which would never meet the lips or mind of another again, for whom I was the last observer and the final obituarist. I read them aloud with feeling and conviction, in such a way as to understand the place of each individual word in the cuneiform text and each line's meaning, both separately and in their place in the whole; they deserved that pastoral care one more time. Some texts wanted to be whispered, as if spoken to a lover, others shouted, like a proclamation or call to arms, and more still to be spoken calmly and clearly, wishing only for the reader or listener to understand them. They each had their own language, different rites and needs, but one never quite understands what that means until faced with the task.

'You'll get better at it the more you do it,' my sister told me when I returned. 'It is something you must feel, but it is a feeling you have to train. As much as we speak about doing it the *right* way, the truth is, with a lot of these stories, there is no right way. There is just the way you read it.'

'I just hope,' I said in earnest, 'I hope if humans ever heard my reading, they'd think I did it justice.'

'I'm sure they would have.'

---

scholars (see. Burkamen *The Funeralist as Echoes of the Past*) point to other Before writings connecting the afterlife to light and death to the dark, this is hard to reconcile with the context of books and stories—which rarely feature in these other writings, other than as a secondary method of remembering the fallen. In this context, the exact meaning of the liquifying and hardening of the wax is difficult to say.

'It comes so naturally to them.' I looked out across the land, then up to the sky in which humans could see everything, anything. 'They say there's a snake up there, marked by those five stars. I can't see it myself, unless I squint, but apparently one day it will eat the world. Is that true?'

'Only sometimes.'

They had such wonderful imaginations, drawing stories out of the aether like that. At the time, I only saw the winged horses chasing the moon, the lovers reaching out to each other, and the netting cast out for fish. Now, I see the war-forged chariots, bloody spears and arrowheads, the calls to war. I see blood and death made destiny.

My tablet spoke of a young girl who married a poplar tree on the edge of the Euphrates. As the old tree grew, it bent over the river and became a bridge, and the young girl became the first to cross it. Her bones became the nails that kept the bridge from falling apart while her blood tainted red the reeds on the river's fringe. It was first love, then blood and bones, that bound the two banks of Euphrates together.

Imagining the girl extending one final, quivering grasp and the tender branches unfolding to meet her, splitting down to the wick, I had to stop myself else I would have cried on my first job out.

'You're too emotional,' my sisters said. 'No wonder they don't let you out.'

Perhaps they were right, but when the alternative was to tell this girl's story and come away undaunted and unchanged, being overly emotional was shorthand for being willing to feel. I steadied my wings to a cool teal, took in a deep, controlled breath, and pushed the tears back to the corners of my eye.

'*Anu granted the girl the totality of affections,*' I read. I had to tell her story in a way that let her be heard, not for what she did but her love and sacrifice. '*She lay in her dying, reeds growing from the marrow of her bones. The sands were without comfort and became fruitful. One tender branch in her palm—*'

I had arrived too early. I knew it in my wings. Not by much, but there was still someone who was to know the girl's story, and only then could I eulogise. The tablet's job was incomplete.

A story never ends till the last person reads it.

I swore under my breath. First assignment out and I was already screwing up. I scanned the room by the bronze light of my candle.

A stone dislodged somewhere behind me. Reflexively, I darted behind the tablets and dulled my glow as much as possible.

A young boy emerged from a crawlspace in the wall between two of the larger tablets. He paused, surveying the inside of the library before making his way around the fallen debris—towards me. Each step was cautious and curious until he stumbled into one of the clay tablets. It shattered on the ground. I flinched. The child held his breath and hunched his shoulders. He looked around as if afraid his father might strike him for his carelessness before closing in only the point of light cutting through the darkness.

What of my candle? I could not extinguish it, not halfway through the ritual, but neither I could do anything to stop the boy reaching it. If he snuffed it out or knocked it into the sand like he had just done to the tablet, the whole ritual would be in jeopardy. So many of my words, painstakingly read, were already inside the little flame.

He called out to me. 'You are in the forbidden place!'

I said nothing.

'You must not come here!' he said, his voice echoing.

And yet here you are.

No scrolls or tablets were forbidden to my kind, and that made him a hypocrite, didn't it, dropping in and interrupting like that? It was the first time I noticed how these remarkable creatures could also be bumbling, frustrating fools, but I wrote it off. I did not know what to make of the boy's behaviour and conjured up a million justifications to absolve him of any responsibility for destroying the tablet. None of them were perfectly convincing. I prayed for him to wander off, but he didn't.

When the child reached the candle, he didn't knock it over or blow it out. He dashed his finger through the flame, first quickly, then slowly, testing how long he could withstand the heat before recoiling with a twitch of pain and a yelp. The firelight only brightened his smile. There was a gentleness to the boy, as if he knew my little candle was important and did not wish to hurt it, even cutting his own laughter short and covering his mouth to ensure he did not blow it out by accident. The tiny flame bent and flexed, then stood up straight. This was the humanity I had heard of. Did the boy understand the gravitas of my task on some level, perhaps even better than I did?

Joy transformed into wonder when he looked up at the tablet my candle was illuminating. The slightest golden twinkle, a reflection of the runes in his soft eyes, crystallised in my mind. This was the last time the girl's story would be read, and there was something magical for me in witnessing that. I was transfixed. Whatever the boy thought of the girl and her boreal lover bleeding on the edge of the Euphrates, I could not say, but I saw earnestness and the part of it he would take with him. I saw the constellations humans made for themselves from nothing but points of light in the night sky and scrawled symbols in fired clay, and as he lightly brushed the dust and sand away to read more, I knew the story had reached a better end.

I may have misjudged my arrival, but any frustration or fear inside me softened. The boy turned away. He paused at the crack to steal a look back at the candle before he crawled through. Perhaps in that small moment, when I slipped out from behind the tomes, he saw me as well. What would he have seen? A flitter of colour against the black? A wavering of air amidst the stillness?

I finished my eulogy.

The library would be rediscovered some two-and-a-half thousand years later, but in that time, much of it would die. In a way, the people kept in those pages would perish anew as all their laughter and songs were lost. I knew of graveyards for the body, but the library was a graveyard of the mind, soul, and spirit. Why would creatures so remarkable, who—like that little boy—read with such wonder, who could build and write such beautiful things, let themselves forget? The library was a way of bypassing forgetting, but they forgot the library.[2]

What would the library say about those who let it die? The questions confounded me at the time, though not as clearly as I have written them here. They came to me as a myriad of feelings and pains: the boy's eyes imprinted on my memory, the last lines of the girl's poetry, and sand falling between my fingers at the end of all things. I only knew I hated the idea. That there was an end at all.

I decided there must have been good reason for the forgetting. Bigger, darker reasons that worked against their nature which I could not understand, and that surely my sisters did after all their years eulogising. Later, I asked my sisters what those reasons were, and they laughed.

The candle winked out and darkness closed in. A wisp of sweet smoke unwound into the air.

* * *

The year was 1938 CE.

The smell of blazing memory left a deep impression. Burning ink, smouldering leather bindings, smoking

---

[2] This line has been the subject of scholarly debate for some time, given the text's survival beyond the Collapse. Whether the text survived accidentally or intentionally—sent forward as a kind of message or warning—or purely by chance is unknown. *The Funeralist's* author seems to lament and knowingly confront the collapse, and it was found in a capsule that some could consider a 'library'—perhaps a method of bypassing the Collapse. Needless to say, it remains one of the most important and complete texts on the Before.

vellum, and paper turned black and ugly in a smoke that lingered in the sinuses. I wrinkled my nose, pinched it, but the scent had already wormed inside and refused to leave. Book after book was tossed into the fiery maw, to an inferno that only grew more ravenous with every work the crowd eagerly fed it. A monstrous, contorting thing that cared nothing for what it was destroying, only that it kept feeding, and it danced for the jeers of the people around it. A poisonous righteousness filled the air. The crowd, much like the flames they served, only grew bolder and more raucous with every book. The fire coughed up ashes so intensely I and my sisters were forced to land. For how large it was, the pyre provided surprisingly little light. Ash blacked out the sky.

In my sweeter and more naive days, I left eulogies like this to my brothers and sisters. They handled them better than I did. I always ended up on the verge of tears and lost my way with words, but some days there were too many, and all at once, and my sisters and I were all needed. It began with just a few of my sisters, but the numbers kept climbing and the fire grew larger. How many of us were there that night? I cannot remember now. My sisters seemed as numerous as the embers in the sky.

'Come, we must go,' my sister had told me.

'All of us?' I asked.

'All of us.'

There were few processions like it.

The horror of our purpose there dawned on me only slowly. Several centuries before, I watched an earthquake level a city and bury ten thousand books under a field of rubble. In 1647, I spoke for the last copy of *Loves*

Labours Won, lost as the *Methuselah* was steered into a storm—lost to carelessness, to erring. I had seen love letters destroyed in hopes of erasing the past. I had not seen this.

A little boy, no older than nine, pushed through the crowd to the front just to cast his father's tattered diary onto the heap and watch it burn. He could not throw it far and retreated from the fires too quickly, so it landed on the edge of the burning mound, merely smoking. Despite this, the other men and women around him cheered him on like a proud parent might their child in a race.

'Kick it in! Kick it in! Go, now!' they urged, and the boy darted in to kick it further. 'Good boy!'

The book quickly caught alight, his father's private recollections and thoughts adding to the acrid taste, cloying odour, and lingering smoke.

Worse than that, I could see the same glee, wonder, awe, and sense of history I saw in the eyes of the boy in the library all those centuries ago etched into the lines of this new boy's face before the bonfire. It was wrong, how wrong. A paradox. I wanted to tear any book from his hands, rip the expression from his face, and instruct him on how to feel. *Be like the boy from the library*, I would have said, and he would not have known what I meant.

'I don't understand,' I told my sisters. 'What am I missing?'

And they told me, 'You are not missing anything.'

'Does he not know what he's doing?' If that boy in the library knew better, shouldn't this boy, as well?

'He does.' My sister's tone was stone cold.

All my life, I believed there had been something special in that boy's eyes, something magical and precious humanity possessed and I did not which set them apart from and above me, which let the little boy see what I could not. Yet seeing the same eyes in this other child before the fire, watching it all burn, told me if those eyes held anything at all, it was something terrible. The only other option was they meant nothing. A façade. Anything special I remembered from the boy in the library was just a memory I had fabricated. A thing of beauty I held so close for so long, taken from me by a little German boy tossing his father's diary into the fire. Perhaps the boy's father had been a dissenter, and he was simply ridding the world of him in this new graveyard of memory.

Have you ever watched an animal die? Not of old age and in their sleep, not surrounded by loved ones, but in the wild with a broken, unhealed ankle after stumbling into a ditch, their leg trapped under a fallen tree, or starving to death and terrified by a fate they do not understand. They cannot move, they cannot eat, and they do not know why. If you move them, it causes them even more pain, and then what? You cannot fix their broken body, and their broken body means they cannot fend for themselves. Prolonging their suffering seems cruel, but taking life is beyond you and not your decision to make, even though the animal cannot make that decision either. Instead of standing over them, you kneel beside them, as if coming down to their level might bring them some comfort. You imagine every twitch of their pain as your own; you take it into yourself and incorporate it into your being, and it wrenches at every lever of feeling till you cry, and you want to cry. You want to feel the vicarious pain because it is the only metric of empathy you can offer.

It was like that. All I could do was feel a part of me burn up with every word, line, and memory as the crowd cast them, helpless, to the inferno—many after such short lives and being read by so few. The boy's father wrote about the first day he brought his son home, and I felt the soft cradle of his arms, about the oak tree on his street and how children pelted each other with acorns, and I flinched with the pain. It was all ashes and smoke and embers in the air.

My sisters and I squatted atop the roofs and lampposts and watched in silence, in solidarity with all their broken spines.

After all my years and feeling so much, I developed a carapace to keep from crying whilst on the job. Crying happened afterwards, if at all. However, there was not enough room for what I was seeing in my body, and it came out in a line of moisture at the bottom of my eye. I did not sob. I did not want my sisters to look, but my cheeks went wet with silent tears. I wiped them from my face with my wings. My sister asked if I was okay, and I told her the smoke was intense.

'Why do they burn them?' one of my younger sisters asked. Her first night out was not so gentle as mine.

'We may not always understand, but we serve anyway,' another said.

I scoffed privately. How could they look on? How did they erase the guilt, hiding it behind greater plans?

The crowd left a simmering mound of ash and embers behind for us. Everything had been purged. Back in the library, I thought about reconstructing the tablets from their fragments. The wind scattered most of the books from the pyre in a million pieces, but we spoke for what we could. Anyone passing by would mistake us for dwindling embers. I lit my candle.

I expected the man's diary to be a political manifesto, a treatise on democracy or social economy that made it so objectionable, but most of the book was dedicated to his son. It began with his birth, detailed his first days in school, and spoke of the time the boy broke his leg and father tended to him. In the later pages, the man wrote of a better world he hoped to build and lamented the wrong road he had taken to it.

'Ironically, everyone remembers the banned books,' I said to the diary. 'They make a point of it. Only the forgotten ones truly die. "I see war the way I see the sun rise in the morning: it comes, and it comes in the same way I have seen before,"' he wrote, and went on to say he wanted nothing of it for his son after the last war. He wrote of how the little boy was already learning to bear arms and kill, being moulded into something he did not recognise as his son. '"I do not know how to speak with him. I do not know how to love him."' What words could I offer that would mean anything? 'It wasn't out of carelessness or forgetting, like so many others. It was in spite of his caution, his care. Only well-loved books died here. Only beautiful ones. Ones loved so much and so fiercely that others had to hate them.'

I was the last amongst my sisters to leave. Our candles all went out but mine. I could not leave because the eulogy did not feel finished, the issue not closed, and something inside me unresolved. A hate I had not felt before was a lit pyre inside me, a hate I had nowhere to put, that no words in my eulogy could ease, and which my candle could not burn away. It ate away at the edges of other thoughts. I wanted that little boy to walk out in the morning under a new sun and see the dark blotch of ash which scarred the pavement—which *he* had left in the world. I wanted the little boy to be left scrubbing it with a mop and hot, soapy water but never be able to erase the mark of his actions so all who ever walked through that square in the ages to come would see it and know what he had done. What they had all done. And as time went by, as the boy became a man, I wanted him to never be able to wash his hands of the ash-black stain. That way, a tint of it would remain forever in the creases of his palms, so that for all that boy had tried to rid the world of these books, so long as the stain was there, a part of those stories persisted, and it would always be the part they hated most, what they 'objected' to that needed to be 'purged'. I prayed they hated that, till one day, that man would become old and die, and the stain would outlast him, as well. Shame. I wanted *shame.*[3]

---

[3] The juxtaposition between this first and second tale is clearly intentional. The poetic symmetry—between the boys, between the 'looks' in their eyes, between the tablets and books, as well as the junior now turned jaded—suggests *The Funeralist* may have been a cautionary tale rather than an account of true events before the Collapse. Was *The Funeralist* a real person? I choose to believe so. The later accounts would otherwise seem strange. What we can say is the world before placed especial importance on transitory knowledge keeping. The idea of destroying knowledge is abhorrent. As Professor Illeui Illeui notes, we do have some things in common with those from the Before. Like the Funeralist, we choose to preserve what we can.

* * *

The year was 2027CE.

The hate stayed with me. It didn't burn as violently as that night in 1938, but it was always simmering, and it took on new forms: bitterness, resentment, and loathing. Little things I had written off as quirks for humanity began to frustrate me, and things that made me uncomfortable, I came to loathe.

A wealthy heiress refused to keep her ancient papyrus scroll in a safe display cabinet, insisting to guests it be in the open air so she could 'appreciate it better with her wine'. Over just a few decades, the humid air destroyed it. She never even had it translated. An old man tripped, broke his hip, and in the process dropped his mystery novel in a puddle of water, eviscerating it. Every year they wrote more and more books, but that just meant there were more to burn and ban—to 'protect the children', 'maintain our culture', 'further our ideas', and other terms people insisted on that meant nothing. Human carelessness and apathy and ignorance—all of it, just by a difference of degree—wrought unbelievable destruction. My eulogies were there to spite them. The gaps between malice and incompetence, incompetence and carelessness, and carelessness and accidents shrunk to nil in my mind.

I became too comfortable with my hate, calling it vigilance or righteousness. The first time I let myself question that was a frosty spring morn in a forest of crowded elms.

Mag-lev tracks cut the forest in half. They ran right past a clearing of tiny button mushrooms which littered the ground like droplets of blood. Pink magnolias were just beginning to bloom, their frosted petals opening to the new sun.

'Pink magnolias were her favourite,' the girl's mother said, and for years afterwards, she would insist they were why her daughter chose that clearing of all places in some vain attempt to draw meaning out of it. After all, the girl had to wander all the way up the tracks to get there and wait for the next mag-train to come. It was in the middle of nowhere.

I arrived only moments after the daughter threw herself in front of the mag-train. I felt nothing for the girl; she was just another fleck of ash on the mound of human suffering. I was there for a scrap of paper, not her. She had stood on the tracks with it scrunched in her hand so tightly her knuckles turned white, clinging to something I could not see, but in the moment of truth, as the train screeched on its brakes, the wind ripped it from her hand. It landed deep in the forest where nobody would ever find or read it.

Her friends never learned why. That was lost on the paper. She was turning fifteen in a month, and perhaps if she had waited till then, when the spring had passed and the pink magnolias had wilted, she may have never gone through with her plan. That was what her mother said. Hypotheticals gave people nothing but false hope, but still hope. Alternate realities to occupy temporarily.

Thousands of years moulded me into a well-oiled eulogising machine: poignant, efficient, all edges and no softness. I set up my candle—which by this point had burned down to an appropriately ugly mess of wax—and lit it with a snap of my fingers. I barely noticed the flash of heat. Any nervousness I had when I first started had been replaced by habit, instinct, and rhythm I could fall back on.

Only, what I read in the girl's note plucked at strings inside me I did not know were still playable. I will not repeat her words here. It would not be right. Did she know the note was ripped from her fingers at the last moment? What did her final heartbeats feel like? That prospect alone gave her words new layers and horrors I had not felt on first glance, and when I read them aloud, I realised I was not doing them justice.

I closed my eyes, reminding myself of the glee on that little boy's face at the book burning, of entire languages stamped out by the march of 'civilisation', of the words spent on war and blood. My sisters gave humanity the endless benefit of the doubt—the benefit of denial—but I would not.

Yet, something got through to me. For every line, word, and meaning I took in, I could not help but see the girl behind them, first as a silhouette, then textured with all the colours of life. One of the first lessons we learned as eulogisers is length dictates little of meaning, and that half page may as well be a several-hundred-thousand-word treatise. I could not capture her intention with instinct or rhythm; no, I had to *feel* it again, like I had back in the library with the girl who died on the banks of the Euphrates River.

I knelt there in the glade, reading her words over and over, and they took root in me.

Every re-read revealed new hopes, regrets, fears, horrors, reliefs, and breaks—feelings all the way down in infinite regress with layers and textures, a Library of

Babel contained within a fifteen-year-old girl. The half page was not made up of lines and words and paragraphs but the strings of humanity that made up this little girl. No, there was no line, no distinction between her and that page, and what was I meant to make of that?[4]

'She wrote you out seven times before she was happy,' I began for my last attempt at a eulogy, but my voice was already wavering. Tears I had not shed in decades were returning. 'Every word had to be perfect, as if by having the right pattern of letters and full stops, you might convince her parents and friends it was not their fault, that they should not worry, and that they should be thankful she's gone. She was determined to leave an explanation, an explication, where her sister hadn't, as if that had been the reason for the devastation left in her wake. So much entrusted to one so little. Maybe you would have succeeded if they found you.'

Hypotheticals, again.

A part of a person dies with every page, but few had so much of a person as that one.

Even as I whiffed my candle out, I could not escape the feeling there was some layer I had not identified,

---

[4] Our knowledge of the 'humans' from the Before is very limited and largely derived from speculation, but one thing remains a theme in the documents which survived the Collapse: humans think of themselves rather highly. They mark themselves out as special. Even in *The Funeralists,* which is arguably one of the more sceptical documents to have survived, humans are simultaneously presented as terribly cruel, even demonic creatures *and* as imagineers and divinely blessed entities. I believe this represented and ongoing debate or crisis that was never truly resolved: are we special or are we ordinary, even unremarkable?

some room in that Library of Babel I had not found and addressed appropriately. Had that always been the case? Had I missed much in my past eulogies? Doubt took me back to re-examining my uncountable eulogies over the centuries.

No. I drew a line. This girl, this note, was different. I fluttered my wings with frustration, washing myself with a myriad of colours and settling on none.

I knelt there in that glade with the button mushrooms and pink magnolias until her body was found. A maglev engineer discovered her first, coming by to inspect the stretch of track that had set off an alert. The police arrived second, and her parents after that. The mother froze at the sight and wailed the long wail of someone who had seen this before. They thought the mushroom caps had been sprinkled with blood, but I could see the difference. The mushroom caps were patterned and soft, their red a shade of bright cherry, but real blood was dark, messy, and discarded with no rhyme or reason. The real blood echoed the violence of how she hit the ground.

'Did she leave a message?' was all her mother said.

I know the note was not meant for me, but I cannot help but wish it were, so the young girl would know someone saw it and heard her.

* * *

The year was 65689 CE.

One by one, books and holotexts closed for the last and final time as the Waning Years swept the galaxy. Our numbers dwindled with humanity the way we had grown with them, as even we were running out of beginnings, middles, and endings. We did not know how to face that, and I still don't. You say goodbye, and they are gone, but never like this. Every time I eulogised for a book, I could see its last moments before they happened, the final time their pages would be turned, which words would be their final ones, but not so with my sisters. Last words only became the last in the aftermath; last memories are random. I had to face permanence. Perhaps I should have eulogised my sisters, told their stories by candlelight.

My sisters and I followed humanity to their last holdouts—from their cradle on Earth to their mining stations on Luna, their spinning asteroid habitats, and colonies across the moons of Jupiter and Saturn, the last surviving of which was a little family dome on Europa. There were hundreds of books there, but most of them had already been eulogised—books like *The Zuo Zhuan* by Zuo Qiuming or *The History of Bees* by Maja Lunde, which sat on the shelf, unopened but looking impressive. Empires had risen and fallen a thousand times, but books endured.

'Go, sister,' my oldest friend said. We were amongst the last few.

'You would entrust this to me, even after all this? There are others more qualified, older, who do not have the complicated history I do, my spite, especially when—'

'Sister, I would entrust this to you *because* of your spite. Few read words like those forced to see the people behind them.'

I had kept my hate in a little satchel at my side. I could pull it out whenever I needed to, but I could put it away as well. It was a well-organised, regimented hate that rarely went unchecked. When a father burned his daughter's books because she dared to read, when a fighter jet bombed a school as 'critical military infrastructure', or when poor regulations saw a flash flood to destroy a library—there I took the hate out and wielded it well. The hatchet remained unburied; it remained in my hand with blood dry along the edge.

Murals covered the metal walls of that dome on Europa: drawings, sayings, and stories which made up the life of the family that lived there. It was not a book in the conventional sense, lest each wall or room be a chapter or page, but it told a story, nonetheless. One learns to recognise them in all their forms, not unlike the Ashurbanipal's library, where they used entire walls for their paragraphs. For how far humanity had grown from their cradle, they always came back to writing on walls, and I always came back to read them.

The collage told their story. A mother, a father, an eldest daughter, and two sons—one of whom was an infant. Drawings of earth were scattered across the walls like droplets of green and blue dashed across a canvas, and clearly the children had been told stories of What Had Once Been. It must have sounded mythic to them, living in that tiny dome, an old fairy-tale world full of breathable air with animals and rivers everywhere—something more than the Infinite Dark.

Their stories of Earth mixed the real with myths and legends. Dragons seemed as real to the children as moose two times the height of a human or cockroaches which could live without a head, and what was the harm in letting them believe such things? Not even the parents knew quite what was true of the past anymore. Perhaps there were dragons back on Earth. It was all so far away, so mixed up in memory and hope, that there was no way to test their theories. Some of the epithets on the walls were so old they had forgotten the meanings, but the words must have had some sort of ritualistic significance, like they only remembered they *were* important, but not *why*.

There were diaries about how to raise children—rules they tried to stick by. I was old enough to not only have read the many iterations of 'spare the rod, spoil the child', but to have been there the first time a man put it down on a vellum scroll thousands of years ago after an altercation with his son. The meanings changed too. In this family, it meant a child could be raised correctly without striking them. From wall to wall of the hexagonal room, they wrote of the harvests, of their new-born son, and of their explorations outside. It made an epic of their life on Europa, decorated with childish drawings that detailed the events further. Together, they watched Jupiter turn overhead through the great glass ceiling, till one day, as I moved from wall to wall, the story changed.

A metal beam was marked with the heights of the children over time. Each of them kept growing—until they didn't.

The father disappeared from the family drawings first. The writing for that year changed hands to the more refined scrawl of the eldest daughter.

'The rocks fell, and dad was under them. We couldn't get to him, but we could hear him, till we couldn't,' it read. A drawing depicted a man buried beneath a mountain of stone.

The mother, bless her, persisted, but Europa grew colder and more hostile, cut off from the inner colonies, and soon she ran dry of milk. Illness took the infant. The babe disappeared from family drawings, and expressions on the other faces went with them—merely blank instead of chalky smiles.

Again, the penmanship changed. This time to a younger and less refined lettering. Spelling was hit or miss, and grammar was done away with. The middle child.

'she sed she wos fine she sed to go away I went away and she then she fell on the ground' it read. No drawings clarified what that meant. They were eulogising in their own way, pulling together all the strings they had to make sense of all the death. That I could understand. That I knew well—all too well by then.

It wasn't the best eulogy, but I gave them credit for trying.

The hand changed one last time. The strokes were finer and more precise, nothing like the erratic scribbling of the children that came before. It could only be the mother's hand, having outlived each of her children. The final drawing depicted her last child ascending, as if taken up into heaven without violence or brutality, without a care and leaving all this behind for a better life amongst the stars. Perhaps he was heading off to find that Earth full of the fire-breathing dragons and headless cockroaches and gigantic moose he had dreamed so much about.

The mother's loneliness lingered. However she died, her fate was not recorded.

'It seems fitting that humanity left behind a fairy tale—a dream of their old life here, of death too, but also of hope. You gave them hope they might be remembered. By whom, they neither knew nor cared. Remembering mattered more to them.' My wings flickered neon pink. My candle was a small courtesy, but there was something to be said about a little light in the dark. I took a deep breath. That family, in their small, hexagonal dome on Europa, had lent towards the light. 'Now, you can rest. Humanity could burn a million million books and would inevitably use that to tell a trillion stories more, but there are none left to erase you.'

The hate left me, but in its place, there was something more complicated.

I blew out the candle.

* * *

The year is Ω.

Time is compressing with s p a c e . The universe is contracting around me. My sisters are gone. My fingertips are pitch black from lighting my candle countless times. It burns indefinitely low. It is finally a haggard, drooping thing, much like myself.

I have seen many beginnings, I have seen the end, and I have seen all that lies in between. I do not know what it means. I thought I did. I still see the boy from the library in my mind, and the boy at the pyre. In 1912, Robert Falcon Scott wrote in his diary, 'For God's sake, look after our people,' and closed it for what he believed was the last time—believing nobody would ever read it. The

Antarctic ice took his expedition, but his diary, his story, found its way to museums across the world.

I hope we suffer the same fate.

That over this final horizon, someone will learn of us in the universe to come, and they will write more books, and my story will not end here.

Now, I can rest.[5]

'The Funeralists' or 'Hate in Five Parts'
by author unknown
translated by Prof. Illuei lluei
dated to Ω of the Last Iteration
preserved by the Maquezqi Library
See attached commentary files.
Please direct questions to Prof. Illuei Illuei in room 322

---

[5] It is this final section, sometimes referred to as the Denouement, that excites perhaps the most debate. Did the Funeralist know the nature of the Collapse? Some lines suggest so. It seems almost prophetic otherwise. Is the Funeralist the author or are they a fictional representation of the author. The account appears biographical but clearly invokes common structures in other myth and fairytales. Either way, the document survived into our universe, as the Author intended, and remains one of the most fascinating remnants of the Before.

Roger, Go at Throttle Up

First published in *ZiN Daily*

Note: every line in this poem is taken from a different person's last words. Font adjusted for visual effect.

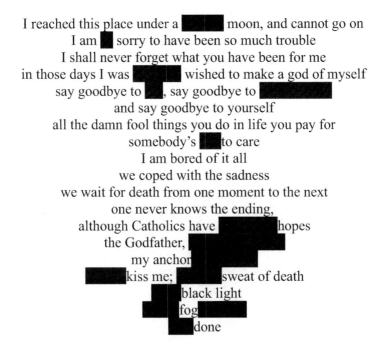

I reached this place under a ████ moon, and cannot go on
I am ██ sorry to have been so much trouble
I shall never forget what you have been for me
in those days I was ████ wished to make a god of myself
say goodbye to ██, say goodbye to ████
and say goodbye to yourself
all the damn fool things you do in life you pay for
somebody's ██ to care
I am bored of it all
we coped with the sadness
we wait for death from one moment to the next
one never knows the ending,
although Catholics have ████ hopes
the Godfather, ████
my anchor ████
████ kiss me; ████ sweat of death
black light
fog ████
done

Waning
so   one who
Pat   the President   got
have their   My archnemesis
is well cast   but don't   it is the
I see   the   is rising   it is

Constellations of Flesh, Bone, and Memory

First published in *Small Wonders Magazine*

Safa knew that twenty-five million years ago, her ancestors decided the forests were no longer for them and left her with a coccyx, the triangular bone structure at the base of her vertebral column, instead of a tail, capable of producing daily bolts of agony and little else for her. She knew that two-point-six million years ago, her ancestors developed stone tools to crack skulls and shells and left her with opposable thumbs—one of which she could no longer feel because of a problem with her nerves. Her parents didn't explain it very clearly. Four years ago, Safa had a small section of her parietal lobe excised—the part that dealt with sensory conditions. It dulled the aches, the pangs when she got out of bed, but not the twitching. Every year brought a new inconvenience, every morning a different decay, as her body refused to recognise itself.

And there she was, back on the surgery table.

'Will it hurt?' she asked the surgeon. 'And you're not allowed to lie to me. I'm not stupid. I know a lot of things. Did you know we get goosebumps because we used to have hair that stood all up and kept us warm?'

'Might be a few body aches while you adjust, but they will pass. We'll give you lots of medication to make you really comfortable after, and you'll be completely asleep before we do anything.'

'Can I see the knife?'

The surgeon hesitated. Other children probably didn't like to think about what was happening to them, but Safa had lived half her life unable to *not* think about it. Every movement was a reminder.

'It's called a scalpel, and this is called a forceps.' When Safa reached out to touch it, she held it back. 'These need to be *perfectly* clean to minimise the risk of infection, and our fingers have all sorts of stuff on them.'

'I know what a scalpel is. What do you with the forceps?'

'It's for holding the tissue while we operate or suture, and if we need to, we can remove some to make it easier.'

Safa also knew that sixteen hundred years ago, in the eleventh century, the Seljuks flooded into the Caucuses, over where Armenia now was. Her ancestors were amongst them, some great-great-great-however-many-parents back, and the Seljuks brought their colourful clothing and art with them. Then, in 1790, the Russian Empire extended its vast, imperial hand over their lands and forced its language down their throats. All of that had been filtered down, through money and time, to the patterns and inscription on the bracelet she wove herself around her wrist. Safa's nervousness came out in absentmindedly pressing it between her trembling prosthetic fingers.

'You'll need to take that off,' the surgeon said, gently moving her hands to her wrist.

For a moment, Safa resisted.

'But you can have it back the moment we're finished. I'll put it right over there, and I'll make sure nobody else touches it.'

'I'm not afraid.'

'I know you're not.'

Even her words and clothes were not fully her own. Safa, like Armenia, grew out of the rubble of Empire.

A couple of nurses soldiered in with cryogenic boxes and hefted them up onto the counter. She could see the odd bits and pieces through glass windows in the side, floating in some kind of gel. How strange to look at them from the outside, not quite part of someone else, not quite part of her.

'All the parts were donated by healthy children,' the surgeon assured her. 'The arms and heart are from a Latvian girl, strong as can be. No more palpitations, no more irregular spasms. And you'll be inheriting a lung from a Laos girl to replace the afflicted one, albeit with a slightly lower volume. Breathing will be a little harder, but no more coughing up blood. You can say goodbye to all of that, Safa. We think this will fix the worst of the symptoms.'

Safa lined her arm up with the one in the container. The skin was a tint lighter and the freckles a little lumpier, but the fingers weren't crooked. The bones all lined up like they did on the posters in all the doctor's offices she had been to. Soon, she'd be one of the patchwork dolls she grew up with.

'Did any of them go to Europa?'

The surgeon squinted through her glasses. 'Sorry?'

'I've always wanted to go there.'

Safa was meant to take the long voyage six summers ago, before her condition set down its roots. Neurologically, her brain refused to recognise her own limbs and organs and was leaving them to rot. Further complications exacerbated the problem. Medication only temporarily prevented her immune system from attacking them directly.

It started with not being able to keep up with the other kids in walks between classes, left breathless and lethargic, but soon the afternoon became a blur, strung from moment to moment, and the itching set in. *Safa, did you hear me? Or does anyone need me to repeat that?* Safa refused to put her hand up when the teacher said that. Her parents tried to make it work. They got her leviter gradus, supervised learning, and alternative grading requirements to make sure she didn't fall behind, but her condition always caught up and overtook her, and Safa had to drop out. Her friends went ahead, and every year, Safa promised them she'd be back the next, but next year never came. It hung over her but always moved a little further back each time. Eventually, her parents stopped promising. So, Safa read everything and anything to stay on top of her learning, as much as she could manage, a scattershot of mathematics and language and especially science.

The condition had been passed down from her mother, who got it from her grandfather, till at some point in the past someone was hit by ionizing solar rays that mutated their DNA, all so that they could pass on what should have been an early death to their descendants. It stayed dormant in their genes, apparently, until it found the 'right' person.

It would have been easier to accept if it were a hover accident, or falling after one of the many times she danced on the fringe of the cliffs near Qusar at sunset—a perfect line of cause and effect that began and ended with herself, but she wasn't allowed such simple arithmetic.

'Acquiring like-grown parts has been complicated recently with the embargo, and matching the legs was difficult, so we resorted to a lunar boy, which is a little closer?' She was prepping while he spoke, her back turned. 'That's the only spacer part we've had to use, but he might have been to Europa.'

'I've never been to the moon.'

'You will soon, I'm sure. Also, we picked them because the hip joints are perfect for yours, but the legs outsize your own by about an inch. You're about the grow a little taller. And you'll need to exercise to build up strength in them before you can walk. Luna only has a sixth of Earth's gravity.'

She liked that a part of her would have been to Luna, and another to Southeast Asia, even though she was no longer sure where she began and where she ended. Would her lung recognise the air there? Would it breathe easier, no coughing? She was always becoming something else.

The surgeons didn't like saying her donors' names, like they were afraid of mentioning that they were real people instead of spare parts that could be swapped and exchanged, but Safa had learned them all—Rūta, Fakru, Sascha, Nalanie—all having died in their own, tragic ways, and she would take them with her to the stars.

'Can I watch?'

'Watch?'

'You could make my body go to sleep, but not my mind.'

She imagined her body being cut open and rearranged, pieced apart and stitched back together in a new constellation of flesh and bone.

'I know it sounds exciting, but it can be a little scary when you see it happen,' the doctor said. 'But if you want, I can send you the recording so you can watch it afterwards?'

Safa nodded.

'What's the first thing you're going to do once you're out? Aside from letting yourself get better.'

'I'm gonna fly to Europa.'

The surgeon's eyes widened and spread to a smile. 'A frontier runner.'

None of her ancestors, none of her new body, had ever ventured out that far. The hinterland of space. She had followed a lot of paths laid down by others in her life, but Europa would be purely her own, footsteps that others would follow someday, and in turn, she would be some small part of them. Fakru would set foot on a new world; Nalanie would breathe new air.

'All the pieces are thawed out of cryo and prepped,' one of the nurses said.

'Are you ready, Safa?'

Safa took one last look at the hands which were no longer hers. Those crooked fingers twitched.

'I'm ready,' she said.

'I'll see you on the other side.'

The operating table was suddenly soft and deep, closing up around her, drowsiness like a blanket pulled up tight around her chest, soothing her, assuring her it was okay to sleep, and Safa swore she could taste the cool Europa air, like water after mint, feel the wet soil between her fingers and the sunlight twenty-five times fainter than on Earth, till even the last pinpricks of the stars, with Europa somewhere mixed in, gave way to the dark and sleep—the tip of her dreams.

A Worm Beneath the Skin

A worm itches under Marama's skin—somewhere between her inner thigh and knee. A skinny creature, twitchy and wriggling, so that when she comes at it with fingernails, it always manages to slither out of the way. It comes and goes, dormant most of the time, but when it wakes, it becomes all Marama can feel, and the itch becomes a burn as her blunted nails scrape across her flesh, red and raw. Tender is good. Tender keeps the worm still, paralysed, fearful of where she might target next. Some nights, Marama goes at it with tweezers and tries to pluck its head out, pluck all the little hairs, ingrown included, leaving a dozen red pinches of flesh. Other nights, she uses wax strips to tear at the whole thing at once. Not one, but three, maybe four yanks before the worm settles down. Then, all she feels is the red burn, like a boiled flannel pressed into her skin, and the worm becomes the least of her worries.

'Did you bring the sunscreen?' Ihaka asks as he handles three of the children at once like a pack of dogs on loose leads. 'The little bottles. I left them on the counter and—oh, God, I forgot the cruskits.'

'You didn't. I grabbed them on the way out.'

Marama digs through her bright blue beach bag and takes out the strangled plastic bottle. She squeezes a dollop of white cream into her palm and begins lathering the children one by one. The good ones wait, eyes closed, grimacing while the oily substance is applied to their skin. The bad ones wriggle, like the worm, eyes on the crashing tide or the other children who are free to roam, hands plying at the sand beneath them, meaning there will surely be patches she didn't get, and the parents will complain when their children come home looking like white and red checkers boards.

'Stay still, Johann,' she insists, 'then you can play. I brought the soccer ball too. Don't kick it into the ocean this time. Or do, and you'll be getting it.'

'Marty steals the ball, he-he-he kicks it away from me,' Johann complains as Marama strokes the lotion over his eyelids. A few smears of white are left, but it's enough.

'Alright, go!' With a little push, the boy rushes down the slope. 'That's the last of them.'

'Now it's just keeping track of them. Don't let Alice wander off this time or they'll never let us come back to the beach. Oliver hasn't put on his rash top yet, but he wants to do it in the changing room.'

'He nervous?'

'He's fine. Sunscreen?' says Ihaka, offering her the bottle while he slip-slop-slaps it down his arms and across his neck. 'It's blistering out here.'

'I already put it on,' Marama says, but she can already feel the lie in the warming sear on her back. Nothing in the way of the sun bearing down on her, burning out the worm.

'Did you?'

'Back at school.'

'Huh,' Ihaka says, pauses, then puts the lotion down and yells, 'Johann! Don't go too far out.' He shook his head. 'Little bastard can't even swim, God. He's going to get us fired.'

'Teacher, lifeguard, bodyguard, librarian, philosopher-king. It's a long job description.'

'I better go out with them. You mind the stuff?' He is already backing away and down the sands before he calls out, 'Oh, and watch Rosetta! She likes playing with the crabs in the rock pools!'

'Got it!'

Rosetta is crouched over a pool some distance from the other kids.

'Rosetta, honey!' Marama calls, and the little kid looks up through her dark curls. 'No touching. The crabs don't like it, and they might nip you, okay? Mamma said no.'

Marama eyes the lotion, picks it up, even contemplates applying it for a second, reminding herself of how her neck will feel lying back against her silk pillow at home and how sunburn will turn it to sandpaper. The blisters that'll keep her from sleeping. She puts it back down, packs it away, and starts watching the children, making sure Kilroy or Magenta or Lackenzie— these new, fanciful names—don't stray too far into becoming a legal hazard.

People don't ask questions about sunburn. Sunburn happens, no matter how bad, even to second-degree burns, and needs not be indicative of anything other than being forgetful or mindless or careless, which are all things she can shoulder. The excuses never run out because everybody gets sunburnt one way or another. Marama isn't ashamed of what she does to her body—this awkward sack of flesh and bone she is inescapably tied to—but she hates dealing with questions and suspicions from people who will never understand the whys. The worm likes the lotion, it's like giving it a little massage, a moisturizer, soothing it in the heat, and she can deprive it of that even if she can't get it out from under her skin.

Marama takes off her shirt and sits back on the towel. She's wearing shorts that expose her inner thigh if she sits at the right angle to the sun. The inner thigh is always a hard place to get. She ties her hair up in a ponytail, exposing her pale neck and all its bulging freckles to the full intensity of the summer sun.

'All of you need to have some water, okay? I don't want anyone fainting. Rosetta! Take a break.' The little girl is wandering over with something in her hand. 'And leave the crab!'

The kids need to stay hydrated on a day like this. They need touch-ups on sunscreen too, especially the kids playing in the water with Ihaka. He plays 'shark' with them, where he dives underwater and chases them, trying to drag them under.

'Where is afternoon tea?' Johann asks.

'You've already had afternoon tea.'

'I didn't.'

'Yes, you did. Go on, a little more playtime before mum and dad come by. You said you wanted to dig a ditch?' She hands him a little shovel, and the kid runs off to start digging.

At the end of the day, parents swing by in sleek Chevys and four-wheeled hybrids to pick up their children till only one is left. It's Oliver, and his mother always comes late because she doesn't finish work till six.

'It's my turn to wait with Ollie,' Marama says.

'You sure?' Ihaka asks, but he is already packing his bags. The question is a courtesy.

'I'll see you tomorrow. Early. And remember the interviews Thursday night. They want to know if their kids are 'special' or 'living up to their potential' or some sh'—she catches herself—'stuff like that.'

The sun dips behind the hedge of trees, winking through the sieve of leaves with bold, golden rays. Ollie sits against the fence, cross-legged and hunched over a pad, drawing cityscapes with towers which lean and reach at odd, impossible angles. He scribbles over any mistakes and draws his second attempt over them, incorporating his mistakes into the design and colouring in the spots with bolder colours. He's always been a quiet kid, but no less inventive. *Children are wonderful creatures.* And they *are* creatures: annoying and chaotic and stop-putting-your-finger-in-there stupid, but Marama had always admired their intoxication with the world and the wonder they could find in the simplest experiences, like a rock pool or a pit of sand.

'You look sunburnt, Miss Dallard.'

'I forgot to put sunscreen on.'

'You didn't put it on the other time either.'

'I must have forgotten then, too.'

'You forget a lot of things,' the boy says.

'There's a lot to remember when I'm taking care of all of you. Did you remember your homework?'

He takes out his green maths book and hands it over.

'Thank you.' She isn't quite sure what to do with it.

'Does it hurt?'

The air is cool, but her neck grates against the fibres of her shirt. They're like barbed wire dragging across her skin, snagging on each of her freckles with little hooks. The crinkle in her left sleeve bites at her arm, and the tag claws at her side. Every movement is noticeable, textured, and all the sensations the brain usually tunes out rise to the surface with twinges of pain. When she feels that, she doesn't feel the worm.

At the angle Marama stands, Oliver's shoulder is exposed. It is flecked with nail marks, like a dozen little pinches of cinched flesh or depressions left where a worm digs into the ground after rain. None seem hard enough to draw blood, but are deep enough to expose the familiar shape of other things. She can only see them standing over him at the angle she is, while he sits on the ground in such a way that tugs at his shirt. No wonder he always wears a rash top.

'Your mum's here,' she says as the crooked little car creaks up the side of the road.

He starts to pack up his things. Does she say something? What is there to say? She could offer him numbing cream or an ice pack to soothe, but she has neither on her. He clearly doesn't want others to know, and offering might mean he goes out of his way to hide it further, or worse, if he's—

Marama puts away the worse thoughts.

Just say it.

'One thing, Ollie. Do you scratch a lot?' She makes sure not to use the same tone she would ask if he finished his homework or shoved some other kid over. Paternalism just made it worse, made it humiliating, like you were a poor wounded animal who needed pity. She has heard it before. Oliver looks at her. She taps at her shoulder. No eyebrows raised, no suspicion.

He hides his shoulder and runs towards the car.

'Ollie, you forgot your maths book!'

He's already inside the car.

Marama leans back against the fence, the scaly wood scraping against her sunburn, and the memory of the first time she plucked hairs from her arm comes to her, unbidden. It rises out of the pangs of pain. When she started out, she did it on her forearm and used her fingers, taking out three or four at once, but people started asking questions—teachers and friends, or those who had been friends—so she got good, she got clever, and she used tweezers, targeting her eyebrows instead. Girls used tweezers to pluck eyebrows all the time, following their mothers; beauty is pain and all that, and nobody bats an eye. A girl plucking hairs from her arm till her eyes welled up was to be stared at, but a girl plucking eyebrows with tweezers till she had to draw them back on was just worried about the boys.

Once through the door and home, Marama strips naked to see the damage. Bold red streaks have matured where her shorts end, and sunburn strafes her back right up to the line of her hair, leading down in a gradient to where the sunlight struggled to reach. Between her thighs, the worm is still and silent, and when she touches her inner leg, all she feels is her dry, tight skin, like plastic wrap pulled tight over a dish of warm meat—rubbery, almost silicone.

It isn't that she sees someone unfamiliar in the mirror, but someone all too familiar, all too her. A haphazardly stitched-together mound of flesh and bone, all angles and fleshy in the wrong places. There are arms and legs which are not quite hers but are attached to her. The blood-red patchwork of her inner thigh—where the worm dwells—stands out. When she lifts her arms to itch her scalp, she is pulling the strings, only they are strings she can never let go of, even if she tries. She wants to shed her skin to see herself underneath. A few strands of hair pull free as she runs her fingers through it.

Marama hisses with pain as she accidentally scrapes her nails across the freshly burnt skin, then again when her hairbrush combs across her red neck. She runs a shower to wash the sand away but has to run it cooler than usual. She sits there, the lukewarm water falling over her, down her neck, and into her mouth. As it flows across her body, rippling over the prickly mounds of flesh between her thighs, she dreams about sleeping easily. Little grains of sand fall away from her body, out of every crevasse and the forest of her hair, to circle down the drain. She finds herself pressing her hand to her inner thigh, pressing the pain as if to hide it.

Sleep comes, then morning, then a scalding cup of coffee, then a traffic jam. Marama hits her head on the wheel, bends her nail back, flinches in pain, and swears, 'Fuck!' Then the light is green, and people are honking behind her. 'Fuck off! I'm going!' The sun is blinding, highlighting the sunburn on her exposed shoulders. The glass in her window magnifies it, somehow, and she leans away to guard against it. The pain is different when she doesn't intend for it to happen. Her car park is taken. Two parents are waiting outside her office.

'I want to ask about the homework they sent home for maths,' starts Mrs William. 'Wilhelm is well ahead of this level. The other children are holding him back.'

'It's important for children to be around other kids of their age.'

'Not if it means they don't live up to their potential.'

'I think Wilhelm is doing very well for his age, and he seems quite happy with where he's sitting in class.' Truth is, their kid isn't even the smartest in her class, not even top five, but she can't say that without upsetting pearls and squash-face here. 'Times tables and fractions extension groups are available, but Wilhelm hasn't quite exhibited the grades expected—'

'Well, he finds the homework easy enough. He blisters through it.'

'I would love to see him share that same enthusiasm in class.'

'It's that Oliver boy. The one he sits with? He's distracting him.'

'Oliver keeps to himself. Thank you, Mrs William, I'll take all this under consideration.'

'I just wanted to make sure he's getting the best schooling.'

I'm sure you do, doesn't quite make it to the tip of her tongue. Instead, she says, 'All of it is being taken under consideration.' Restraint is respect and respect is restraint with these people. She digs her nails into her palm, unblinking, till Mrs William backs down and slinks back into her Hummer. The rest of the night is filled with

'She's very capable when she puts her mind to it,' 'I'm just concerned he's not living up to his full potential,' learning enhancement strategies, disciplinary issues, and dismissive no-fault-of-mine parents. Rosetta peering into that rock pool and pulling out a crab, like a dove in a magic trick, comes to mind. Marama draws a little crab in the corner of her work booklet.

'Miss Dallard?'

'Sorry, Mr Thompson. Come in. Keely is doing very well,' she starts.

The next day starts with handwriting, then social studies, then they are looking at lepidopterans—moths and butterflies. Some kids are creeped out by the grey critters splayed out behind the glass, but Oliver is enthralled, and he carefully plies the wings so as not to tear or damage them, eyeing them close behind a magnifying glass. Once the bell rings, the kids vacate outside, Ihaka in tow to keep an eye on them, but Oliver doesn't move.

Marama sits on the opposite side of the table. The chair is built for children, and she can't sit comfortably no matter how much she readjusts. It is like forcing two incorrect puzzle pieces together: the bones of her butt and the plastic frame of the chair. The frame rubs against her sunburn, even through her clothes, but she grimaces through it.

Across from her, she can see fresh wounds on his shoulder, just peeking out from under his shirt.

She tried talking to kids about issues at home before. Half the time, they never admitted to anything, even when it was painfully obvious. The other half, they pleaded with her not to tell their parents, like they were being caught out for something. Was she on their side? Hard to tell when she has secret meetings with their parents every term, and adults always have their tricks. They seem simultaneously all-knowing, all-seeing, and also dumb enough to miss a kid clearly keeping another kid's lunch under their seat. Truth be told, she finds it harder to care these days. Thirty kids a year come and go, each and every one with a host of their own issues, most of which they will overcome one way or another. Plus, she only has six hours a day with them. Six hours made for three hundred and sixty minutes; divide that by thirty, and you only get twelve minutes a child, at best. She has to fit English, Māori, mathematics, science, and social studies in there somewhere. It isn't that she *wants* to feel this way. It comes to her as exhaustion, repetition, and numbness she had to fight past—to remind herself of Rosetta looking in that pool and of Ollie eyeing the moths.

And so, she finds herself talking.

'Ollie, I noticed something, and I want to talk to you.'

Oliver presses his eye into the magnifying glass even harder to avoid her gaze. It certainly isn't going to help him see the moths. Marama's hands move to the uneven landscape of time-healed scars beneath her sleeves—not from a razor or nail, but from the tip of a 2B graphite pencil. There is a pencil sharpening machine on the other side of the room. She used to wander up to one just like it every hour and carve the pencil to a lethal tip. It started out as drawing pictures in her flesh before it became more, but never looked like anything more to anyone else.

Why do you do it? She could say that, but she hesitates. It feels almost hypocritical to ask. It's the question everyone wants to ask, half for their own gratification and half because they care. The words are motions of caring, the shape and form of it, the sound it makes, and then it's out of your hands. Numbness makes it difficult to tell. The worm is distracting. The more she thinks about Oliver's, the more she feels her own. Marama removes the seat from under her and sits cross-legged on the ground.

Any number of explanations for why they do it spring to mind, all of which are fictional on some level—exaggerating or minimizing some things in favour of others—because a real reason is the only thing she can't truly give anyone. That's why she has refused to share the worm with anybody before. Her mum asks to no avail. People look for sob stories or deep-seated traumas that take root and grow into these ugly, thorny problems, and if you solve those you solve it all, when sometimes the answer is so monotonous and undeserving as to be unworthy of mention at all. If you don't have what they're looking for, then it becomes pitiful, shameful. *You have no excuse,* they think, and that's what they're looking for: the excuse.

Marama stifles a chuckle. She needs to add 'counsellor' to that list in the job description. And therapist, even if she is doing a crap job of it.

'Look, I'm not going to stop you, but I want you to do something.'

He never puts down the magnifying glass.

'That,' she starts, pointing at his shoulder. 'I'm not going to stop you, but next time you want to, I want you to tell me, okay? Just talk to me first, alright? If you need time out of class, we can talk about that. Or if you want to draw a bit more? Maybe some time looking at the butterflies? I don't know what'll make it easier, but if there's something you'd rather be doing, just come talk to me. Not Iha—Mr Glass—just me.'

Oliver traces a finger over the glass above the *antheraea polyphemus*, with its goat-like eyes on its wings and tan colours blending into pink and gold. Royalty pressing right up against the ordinary.

'And you don't have to tell me what's wrong, if someone said something or whatever, okay?' She is desperate just to get the kid to acknowledge her. 'Of course, you can. I'm here, and I'd love to help if you'll let me, but you do have to tell me you want to hurt yourself so I know, and that way, if things get worse, you know you can talk to me because… I get it. Or I don't get it. I don't know what it's like, but you can talk to me.'

She looks down at the hands attached to the end of her wrists and sees thick, bulging fingers, like sausage meat. They throb as if not enough blood can force its way through the narrow passage of her wrist, leaving her palm splotchy, somehow both a vivid red and pale at the same time.

'Can I draw instead of social studies?' Oliver asks, not even looking up.

'You're ahead in that, so I suppose so, but just today.'

The boy finally looks up with one eye bulbous through the magnifying glass.

'Mom says she wishes I was better at school.'

'You do well. I know your grades. You did excellent work on that math homework.'

'She says it costs a lot to come here and I need to live up to my potential.'

Potential. He sure as hell can't spell the word, but he knows it. He knows the weight of it and the gap it leaves, but not how to fill it.

'She might say that, but I know how hard you work,' Marama says. 'Do you feel you work hard?'

'I try to.'

'I think you do. That's all that matters. And sometimes, we can't work as hard, and that's okay too.'

'Are you gonna tell Mum?'

That was the question she feared. Technically, she had an obligation to.

'I…' She is not cut out for this, and she knows the hypocrisy of what she's doing, but nobody else knows, so nobody will call her one.

The bell rings, children pile back into class, Ihaka shepherding them in, and everyone settles into their assigned seats.

Ihaka eyes her. 'You alright?'

Something of it must be written into the lines of her face. 'Great.'

'You look ill. And sunburnt.'

'I think I missed a few spots.'

'Every spot, it looks like.'

The blistering was coming in.

'It's my turn to stay with Ollie,' Ihaka says.

'No, it's fine, you go,' says Marama. 'I have to stay on, anyway.'

'Yeah? Why?'

'Things.'

'Ominous,' he chirps before taking his chance and ducking out the door.

Marama stays with Ollie till his mum pulls up. It's always hard to know what to think of parents. She got such a limited view of them, through drop-offs and pick-ups, filtered through the eyes of their kids and what you could infer from their behaviour. Ollie's shoulder doesn't make his mother evil, but it certainly complicates Marama's feelings towards her. An ambiguity opens up between them which she can't quite close or rest on too heavily. Before he leaves, Ollie smiles at Marama. Does it represent a promise? A thanks? An apology?

A traffic jam keeps Marama from reaching home before seven. Dinner is soba noodles, spam, chilli jam, and wilted greens of questionable quality. They had been lying in the fridge for a touch too long by the taste of them, but she hadn't the appetite to care about what went in. As she stands in the kitchen slurping a long, cold noodle, she catches her reflection in the night-blackened glass of a window. Her body is made of a dozen bloated pieces of meat, and the worm is back, crawling up her thigh just under the skin, chewing on the fat. It's cold enough the sunburn does nothing. She puts her bowl down and tries to push the worm from her mind.

She starts itching at her thigh absentmindedly, stopping every time she catches herself, swearing it off and rubbing her skin to numb it—not permanently, never indefinitely, but for a minute or an hour because those are manageable. She can see the end of them. But the worm keeps burrowing into her skin. It finds little passages under her flesh. It pulls strings inside her to make her feel ill. When the hour is up, she allows herself to scratch at it again until the skin chafes, and she can lie back in a wash of relief, like the first moment an addict gets their hit and for a brief second, they do not question doing it. It never lasts.

Her legs lift her up off the couch, take her to the bathroom, where her hands find the little metal tweezers. Running on something pre-programmed, her fingers guide the implement to pluck at the rawest stretch of her own skin till blood streaks down her leg. Anyone would think she was on her period. Her inner thigh has been stripped of leg hair, each one painstakingly plucked out, but she takes up a wax strip. Tearing off the smooth back, she slaps it across her leg and—without bracing, without a deep breath, but with the compulsive, axiomatic, and insatiable reactivity of a well-oiled algorithm run a thousand times before— yanks it off. A second time, a third, a fourth, a fifth, a sixth, a seventh, an eighth, a—

Marama slumps onto—no, into—her bed. Every fibre of the duvet, every crease in the blanket, and every slight movement she makes takes on a hyper-reality. Every sensation of rough, smooth, grainy, fluffy, and coarse are made ten times more potent than before, such that she can feel the gaps between the hairs on her arm and every movement as she breathes. The tiny creases in the sunburnt skin of her neck, where the flesh has just started to crack and peel, reveals even more premature layers underneath. The involuntary twitches of her legs catch texture and feeling where they never usually would. These things are usually drowned out by the persistent numbness of the day to day. It's like suddenly becoming real again, and the world isn't paper-mâché.

The worm, wherever it is, retreats into the oily, fatty recesses deep inside her body.

'Hypocrite,' Marama whispers.

She sits up on the edge of her bed, the duvet scrunched between her legs and pressing up against her inner thigh, for a good ten minutes. The word lingers in her mind. *Hypocrite.* It doesn't carry the weight of an accusation. It lacks the sudden realization, the how dare you, the *am I?* It feels like a word someone would use when they don't really know what they're talking about, or when they have a one-dimensional understanding of the situation. Yet, at the same time, it isn't like Marama can fully explain her own emotions to herself. Her feelings *are.* She *is.* That's about as far as it goes, but that doesn't make it okay.

'Hypocrite,' she says, as if sounding out the syllables would make each of the constituent parts clearer.

She expects this of Ollie, and he would expect the same of her. She wants to expect the same of herself, but can't quite get over that line—not permanently, but she does tonight. Even if only through the anger at herself, even if only momentarily.

For him.

She reaches for her phone on the bedside table and brings up her mum's number. When Marama tells her, she will want to know the *why*, everyone does, even if she can't give it. Not a concrete one, not one that would satisfy that desire. Until she has that answer, it feels hollow to call—only she knows that isn't true on some level, even if she can't quite buy into it. She's meant to believe calling will help, and so, she chooses to believe it.

Marama touches the tender flesh between her legs, flinches, and dials the number.

On the Beach of Forgotten Things

'The Beach remembers.'
— The first Lighthouse Keeper

The Lighthouse crouched out on the craggy lurch of land at the end of the Beach, its antiquity visible in its silhouette—a melting candle, burning low. It could ward off ships from the jagged rocks but do nothing to fend off the bitter wind, the last vestiges of a distant storm over the Sea. It was a wind that made Esme's teeth ache as he picked through the sands with his driftwood staff. Searching, always searching. A wind as cold and brutal as this meant new memories washing up on the shores.

He was humming an old song in a long dead language with lyrics which cannot be written—a song which all the world but he had forgotten—when his staff caught on something solid under the sand. White foam was washing about his Wellingtons.

The old man knelt down, leaning on his staff. His knees crackled with complaint, but he scooped aside the muddy sand to reveal a rusted pocket watch. It wasn't doing a very good job at being a watch anymore given the hour hand was bent out of shape by an overly zealous raccoon, but it wasn't like time passed on the Beach anyway, so Esme wasn't one to complain.

A young boy had been sprinting through a walkway some miles south of Norfolk when the pocket watch fell from his side into the greenery. The raccoon picked it up and hauled it back to its cosy den: a discarded trashcan. The boy didn't even return to pick it up. He forgot he was even wearing it.

The old man knew these things by mere touch the way the Others, who lived out beyond the Sea, knew how to fall asleep or breathe without thinking, how sailors sensed a storm, or how dogs knew when it was time for a walk. Well, the pocket watch was Esme's now, and there was nobody to complain about it.

Esme clipped the watch to his belt after looping the hand-wrought chain through his pant loops. It jingled at his side as he shuffled down the Beach.

Not long after, he stumbled across a framed certificate for 'Service to People of Charleston'. It would have been a nice gesture if the mayor hadn't awarded it to himself after being accused of tax fraud, misappropriation of government funds, and kidnapping a rather overweight seal named Ronald. After the mayor became no-longer-the-mayor and instead a sour-faced headline for the local paper, the certificate was discarded in some forgotten storage room on a property the council board barely remember it owned. Years passed, and the mayor lived on, but not his certificate, which even he scarcely remembered receiving.

The certificate wouldn't look any good on Esme's wall, so he left it, and the sands took it. The sands took everything in time. Things forgotten and things discarded, the Beach picked up the remains.

The wind had hardened with a sheen of not exactly rain, but wet caught in the air, salt water whipped up by the ripples of that distant storm. Esme pulled up his vivid yellow raincoat hood. It kept out the wet but little of the cold. Not that he felt it much. Cold had been a near-constant companion on the Beach for eons. It was more the extra water weight in his beard he wasn't fond of lugging around, plus having to dry out his clothes every day.

The Lighthouse had been reduced to a glimmer in the distance. Only the warm, ever-burning fire at its top was visible through the haze. It was calling him home with a pot of hot, steaming stew and a roaring fire, but no. He pushed on. He had sands to dig through, relics to see.

By night's end, Esme had collected for himself a couple of love letters from two women who barely remembered each other, the harness of a rather optimistic canyon climber, and a doorknob. The doorknob wasn't anything special; he just needed a new one for the top floor, and this one had a lovely little piglet a toddler had drawn on it. Storms always brought in the best artefacts. They swept up more intense histories, wrung the ocean of its paraphernalia, and dumped it all on the Beach. Sometimes, it took days to work through everything.

He was about to turn back when his staff hit a mound of seaweed.

'Ugh…' the mound of seaweed groaned, so he poked it again. 'Ow!'

He had encountered talking dolls and magic eight balls before but never talking seaweed. What use would that have been to the Others over the sea?

He whacked it.

'Ow! Stop hitting me.'

'I've hit plenty of seaweed before, and they've never complained.'

'I'm not seaweed,' said the seaweed.

'Well, then I'd stop looking like seaweed, love. Probably start with getting rid of the weed.'

A face appeared through the tangled web of washed-up greenery. A real, fleshy face. A girl, no less, young and bright. She blinked a few times. Contrasting with the grey of the Beach about him, the little girl's face was like a freshly picked peach.

'I haven't had a peach in a long time,' he said to himself.

She spoke as if waking from a dream. 'What?'

'Peach. Usually about yay size, the size o' my fist—'

'I… I know what a peach is.'

'Then why'd you ask?'

The girl sat up, rubbing her forearm and ribs where he must have jabbed her. The wee one was drenched to the bone and shivering, but clearly dazed, eyes glassy and distracted. She looked about as if sleepwalking. He must have woken her. She started untangling herself from the seaweed, looping the ropes this way and that before frustratedly tearing them off and discarding them down the beach.

Esme cocked his head, blinked, and pulled out his spyglass to peer a little closer. He could make out the bulbous freckles just below the girl's eyes—laid out like a constellation to his eyes.

He grabbed her arm, lifted it up, and wheeled it around.

'Wonderful range of movement,' he said as he puppeted her. 'I've not seen a doll this realistic before.'

She stole her limb back. 'A d-doll?'

'Girl, this skin is very fleshy.'

'B-because it's flesh!'

'Yes, I'd almost think they skinned some poor fella to make this, and the freckles! Don't even look painted on. There's some real texture.'

He rubbed his thumb on her cheeks, distorting them this way and that to see how far they could stretch before she pulled away. The girl wrapped her soaked cotton cloak about herself. Very convincing. Not that it'd help, of course.

'I'm not a doll,' the girl said slowly. 'Why do you think I'm a doll?'

'Well, you can't be a human. Humans don't come 'ere. Don't belong, no, not 'ere. Less you're me, though I'm not half as human as I was, not since I came to the Beach.'

'What—' She tried to stand, but in doing so, was overcome with dizziness. She buckled over on all four, her face flashing white, and she puked violently into the sand, seawater expelling from her system. Heaving, the doll sat back down, gathering herself till she could push words out between her retching breaths. Remarkable. She even came with bodily functions. He had come across a few dolls like that, but nothing so detailed. 'Wh-what are you t-talking about, old man?'

'It runs off about as far that way as you can run and then a little further, about as far *that* way as you can fly and then twice as far, and don't even try heading inland. The Beach outruns you.'

The girl wiped her eyes and pulled the wet strands of hair from her face. He could smell the salt, sea, and sick on her.

'I... I don't know how I got here.'

'None of you ever do, though not like any of you ever know much or things at all. You must have washed up with the tides, yeah?'

Her shivering had set in violently, and that yanked on just the right strings. Her skin had turned from pale to white, frostbite encroaching on her fingers and toes. The wind had shown its ugliest face, which could turn the cold deadly.

'Girl, take this.' He shouldered off his yellow jacket. The inner lining was thick flannel kept perfectly dry by the waterproof exterior. 'Or the cold'll be the death of you. And get those clothes off, or at least roll 'em up to get them off your skin. The Beach is beautiful, but beautiful don't mean it won't kill you. The water don't want you. The water don't want anyone, not even me, so it spits you all out.'

She took the jacket and changed inside it. Even in the brutal wind, that must have been preferable. It was three times her height, meaning the weight of it dragged along the ground, but it was better than her freezing to death. Certainly, she was the most curious artefact the Beach had ever brought Esme, and definitely worth taking back to the Lighthouse for a closer look.

'Thank you,' she said from underneath the jacket.

The little hobgoblin followed Esme on the path back to the Lighthouse. All he could see of her head was his jacket hood bopping up and down. The wet sand and heavy jacket made for a sore and slow journey, each step of hers sinking a few inches into the sand. Esme had gotten used to it in his Wellingtons, but the girl was in patchy flats at best. Already soaked, her socks couldn't get much wetter than they were, but the sand got into every little crevasse it could. It had settled into a thick layer of grime across her brow. The cold had stolen feeling from her.

The prickly throne of the Lighthouse came into the view. The burning bulb at the top cut through the haze with red, white, and gold, pulsating as it turned. From a distance, the Lighthouse looked to be surrounded by battlements pointing outwards. Esme rather liked that impression. When the lightning struck just right, he was a reclusive vampire in his stormy castle. He lacked the fangs and penchant for haemoglobin, but he had the dramatic cloak whirling down.

'Come now, girl. Not far!'

But the girl had keeled over. What was once a mound of seaweed was now a mound of yellow flannel. He hobbled over and jabbed her a few more times. She didn't move.

'Well, I ain't leaving you 'ere, but you if my knee gives way tonight, it'll be on you.'

He stabbed his staff in the sand for support, knelt down, and picked her up in his arms. Each step was an accident waiting to happen for the old man, but he carried her like a bunch of daffodils back to the Lighthouse.

'The Beach outruns you.'
        — *The second Lighthouse Keeper*

Esme chanced across a half dozen diaries and journals on his way back. Those were a dime a dozen on the Beach. Start them one day, with all the optimism you can muster, before life gets in the way and you put it off, just for a couple of days, before you stop it all together, and then you forget, and the Beach takes it. Everyone tried to do one at some point, and every last one was inevitably left behind someday. In his early days, Esme had rather enjoyed reading them. *He listens in all the right ways* and *if I could tell her how I feel, she might feel the same.* War diaries came in waves, thousands left languishing on the Beach, splayed and torn at the spine, ink bleeding through the pages. *Mom, I want to come home. Mum, I'm gonna die out here. Mom, I'm gonna be home soon. Mom, they say it'll be over soon. Mum, I'm doing my best.* War stories and love stories, all the same in one way or another—people wrestling with how to *live.* Then came the other stories. Something about a set of baby shoes, never worn. In time, Esme had collected them all. He'd need to come back for the interesting ones on the Beach another day.

They reached the cliffs.

'Not long now, love,' he assured the bundle in his arms. The peach-girl stirred lightly.

The path up the craggy layers of the spit wound back and forth, but the rocks shielded them from the bitter touch of the wind. The air remained just as cold, and the peach-girl just as pale.

Esme prodded the mouldy wooden door to the Lighthouse open with his staff. It swung ajar with a yawning creak, and he sidled inside so as to not bang the peach-girl's head on the doorway. The door closed behind them, and the warmth embraced them. He lay her down on the couch. Howling and shuddering made it seem like the Lighthouse was making a final stand against the wind, but Esme had faced the storms a thousand times before and never lost. A fire bustled and chuckled under a stone arch on the opposite side of the room, its light catching on the countless oddities scattered about the space. The fire never died, of course, much like the tides never ceased, and it fought off the cold effortlessly. The air inside was still, bar the minor draft from the fireplace. Esme stoked it with his poker and a log or two, sending up a fount of embers. One settled in his beard. He pinched it with his fingers.

The poor, wee peach-girl was shivering fiercely, her body convulsing to generate what little heat it could. Even though the fire cast her cheeks red, there was no warmth in them. Dead, but vivid green eyes flicked up to him from under lax eyelids, a touch delirious, before she scanned the room. She was chattering.

'Come now, girl, we need to get you warm, but slow.' He knew full well warming her too suddenly could make her heart give out, so he got her out of her remaining drenched clothes and into a woolly jumper. He slipped fluffy socks over her feet. None of what he had fit her. His wardrobe was designed for a man three times her size, making her look like a newborn swaddled in flannel.

'Th…thank you,' she said. Her voice was weak.

Only as he was getting her dry and warm, a piece of paper fell from her fingers. She'd been scrunching her fist closed—to keep warm, Esme had assumed—clinging to this scrap of paper. It fell to the wooden floorboards. She was too out of it to notice. Seawater and sand had worn away at it, but he could make it out: a train ticket. He had seen plenty before. Esme knelt to snatch it up.

The sense of one lost, fleeing, running, hiding, yelling, and slapping filled his mind. He sensed half-hearted hugs, quiet nights alone, the *clink* of empty bottles, and a train station.

He put it on the stool beside her.

Over the next while, warmth returned to the peach-girl. Her ice-white cheeks patched over with rose and her fingers twitched and turned into little red sausages. The little thing began to stir and mumble before falling asleep in his chair. Rain battered at the windows.

'Quiet!' he hissed, and the rain courteously started battering a different window.

Esme got to brewing a stew over the fire. He cut the carrots and celery with a knife that had washed up some centuries ago, from an old hunter who lost his way in the icy northern wilds whilst tracking a reindeer. After a tumble down a slope, his gear got scattered, and he left the knife behind. A steel blade with a bone handle, run smooth after generations of carving up carrots, celery, and presumably reindeer if his father was luckier than him. The Beach picked it up. The ladle he stirred the pot had spent most of its life as a rather inefficient candle holder. Some lord of a little nowhere had tottered about his house with a wax-filled ladle to light his way because he wasn't going to give in to 'Big Candle', who made candles run out to sell more candles. The pot lay atop a stack of photo albums of once happy, now forgotten families, all laughter and frozen moments, till the years went on and the boys became men who could be reaped.

The Lighthouse filled with sweet and savoury aromas, but it was the smell of hot cocoa, rich, deep, and full of comfort, that brought the girl back. It'd been half a day, and the storm was still raging. When she opened her eyes, a mug with little flower decorations, clearly hand-painted, waited on the stool for her. It was so big she needed two hands to pick it up.

'Afraid it's just the smell of hot cocoa,' the old man said with a chuckle. 'A woman was struck with melancholy a few candle collections back and forgot what the hot cocoa from her childhood smelled like. She used to sit on the porch and watch the sunset, all wrapped up, while her Ma made the chocolate. The smell came 'ere on the wind, and I trapped it in that bottle there. It's really just milk, but breathe it in and it might just taste right. Go on.'

Peach-girl took a long, deep breath through her nose as she drank. It wasn't too hot as to burn her tongue nor too cold as to lose the feeling of warmth seeping through her body. It found its way into all the little corners. The old man was right. When she breathed in the smell and drank the milk, it tasted like cocoa.

'Thank you,' she said meekly.

Esme slurped through his bowl of stew, shovelling the contents into his mouth before he noticed the little girl watching him. He choked, spluttered, and put the bowl down. Streaks of it dripped through his beard, which he only saw by the mirror on the back of the front door—

which had been forgotten in a collapsed apartment complex in Versailles. He grunted a 'sorry' before cleaning himself up. Esme's company for dinner was usually a broken cuckoo clock and a metronome, neither of which had much of an opinion on how he ate his stew.

'It's fine,' she said, sipping her drink.

It was only then the girl could really take in the Lighthouse, which could only be described as an overstuffed menagerie of incongruent things. *Things* in the most definitional sense because the whole place was packed with oddities which, in some way or another, seemed just a touch out of place. The cuckoo clock was clearly broken, always on the verge of interrupting. Each and every pot, pan, knife, and fork seemed to come from a different kitchen set—some ornate and refined, while others looked like the product of a child who failed a woodworking class. A thousand lockets hung from hooks on the walls, whilst books seemed to occupy about every bit of space they could, and then a few inches more. The books were from every age and language. It was the library of a polyglot with every interest and yet no specific interest at all. A delicate chandelier hung from the misshapen wood-planked ceiling, like it'd been plucked from some aristocrat's house. In every corner, there was always just a little less space than needed.

She tried to stand up, but the old man raised his hand.

'Easy now, girl. You were out in the waters, and the waters don't want you there. You caught a chill, if not the likes of worse. Can you feel your toes?'

She gave them a little flex.

'Good, good.'

'What is this place?'

'It's the Lighthouse.'

'Yeah, but which lighthouse?'

'The only Lighthouse,' he said, taking another mouthful. 'On the Beach.'

'Okay, but which beach?'

'The Beach.'

'And where is the Beach?'

'Right beside the Lighthouse.'

She sat up a little. 'Are you a crazy person?'

'I'm the sanest person here,' he said.

'Are there other people?'

'Well, there's you.'

'Yeah, but not me.'

'There's me,' he said.

'I don't know what to say.'

'That's okay.'

She screwed her fists into her eyes. Her hunger suddenly became apparent, and she took up the bowl of stew he had provided. She never liked carrots and celery, they made her tongue itchy, but something about this man's stew made it the most appetising thing in the world. Each little morsel was a comfort, each little mouthful the best tasting meal in the whole world. She went slowly at first before gulping the rest down like a sailor on his one day ashore. A trail of glistening liquid was left down her chin. Esme chuckled.

She got up and started perusing.

'What's that?' she asked, pointing to a clunky metal contraption on one of the higher crooked shelves.

'A tippity-typewriter. The woman who owned it tossed it into a river when her novel refused to come together. She tried to retrieve it, but forgot where she threw it in. Poor soul was only a few feet wrong. Holes in the brain, I tell you. Things fall out from time to time.'

'That's sad.'

Esme picked up one of the lockets. It had a picture of a mother and her two children: age had taken the memory of them from the mother. She left the locket on a park bench somewhere, believing it belonged to someone else.

'Sometimes, we remember, aye, but sometimes, they're taken from us forever, even when we care—till it ends up 'ere.'

'And what about these?'

It was a dusty glass frame of pressed flowers and splayed moths.

'A collector died and passed it onto his son,' Esme said, 'but the son hid it away in corner of his attic in some unlabelled, unnumbered box. It gathered dust till it turned to dust.'

'Why?'

'From time to time, we choose to forget. And the collector? He was not a good man.'

The girl gravitated to a small cloth shirt riddled with what could only be bullet holes. They were in the back of the shirt. The shirt must've fit a child.

'What about this?'

'Mm…' the old Lighthouse Keeper started, suddenly less certain. He mumbled to himself for some time before prying the shirt gently from her hands and placing it back up on the shelf, feeling the shape of its past as he did so. 'The truth is, most things are forgotten because we don't care to remember them. We let them fall away, like sand through our fingers.'

Every inch of his walls made for a colourful collage. Where others might've seen his little room as a graveyard, he saw a museum. Alumni of other lives lived, died, and forgotten.

'How do you know all this?' she asked.

'Because I'm the Lighthouse Keeper.'

'And you keep…'

'The Lighthouse.'

Something in that made the girl smile. A ghost passed her face, a memory returning to her. Her eyes went to the crumpled train ticket, and she must have figured out he had seen it. She picked it up with both hands.

'I was at the train station…' She spoke as if recalling something from a dream.

'Ain't no train station at the Beach, not less you know something about the Beach I don't.'

'My Ma, she was there, at the station. She told me to wait while she got things ready. I waited for her, I did. On the platform, just like she told me.' The girl's forehead creased. She squinted, piecing together the memory. 'There were so many people running around. I—I couldn't see her anymore. But then they had the final calling, and Ma hadn't come back for me yet, and the train was leaving. It was leaving so fast, and I ran. I… I ran, I did, but Ma told me to wait.'

The Lighthouse Keeper went to the girl—kneeling to her level. The old floorboards groaned under him. His dark eyes were heavy with age, but they twinkled with starlight when they met hers. In them, she could see infinity. With the care of a child cradling a kitten, he took the ticket from her.

A child lost in crowd. Everything is so big, so wide, and all the people so tall, like she's in a forest. They block out the sun. 'Just stay here,' her mother tells her, and she does. Minutes passed, then an hour, but she stays. She waits. She tries to move but is shoved back by a man jumping onto the train. Her suitcase is caught on a crack in the cobblestone, and it's so heavy she can't move quickly. 'Ma!' she calls out, but there's just the sounds of hissing steam and clunking metal. 'Ma!' she calls again, but the crowds swallow up her words. 'Ma! The train's leaving!' But nobody hears her. She's just another child crying in the station, and people with places to be are swishing this way and that. She chases after the train. 'Stop! Stop!' she cries, and she might just keep up, but it's too fast, and she's too slow. Her little legs trip and her suitcase spills open. Her good blue dress falls onto the tracks. The crowds clear, and she's alone. 'Ma? Ma...?' But her mother was on the train and far away from there, trying to forget what she had done.

'Ma told me to wait...' the peach-girl said.

'What's your name, love?' His voice was half a whisper.

'Asha.'

'That's a beautiful name. My name's Esme.'

'I've never heard that name before.'

'I don't hear it very much either. Keep yourself wrapped up. You can't let the cold back in.'

'I... Everyone else was getting on the train, but Ma hadn't come back for me yet. She told me, "Stay here," so I did, but she didn't come back. Why didn't she come back for me?'

He knew the answer. Whether he had the heart to say it was another question.

'I tried to find her,' Asha said. 'I tried to catch the train, but it was too fast. I ran.'

'The whole world's too fast, love. We never catch up. We just fall behind little by little, more and more, till we're too far gone and fall off the end.'

'I don't think I want that.'

Esme was staring out the window, watching the rain droplets streak down the glass.

'Depends on what's off the other end, eh?'

Asha's eye caught on the mantlepiece. She approached tentatively. An elephant plushie sat against the wall, wedged between an empty glass bottle and a broken, overflowing terrarium. The plushie's left ear had been chewed off by baby teeth, though a puppy had given it a fair go too.

'I... remember this,' she said. 'Pudge.'

'Ah...'

'I used to sleep with him every night.'

'And everyone said you were too old for Pudge. You used to suck your thumb and press his ear over your nose, till all the oils in your face got into the cotton and made it smooth as butter. And you pressed his face into yours so hard his eye got smudged out of place. Too much love. But people told you to grow up, so your Ma put him away in the stairs cupboard one day and didn't tell you.'

The little elephant was in a sorry state, but Asha held him close, careful not to tug on the fragile threads of his ears. His left side was deflated; all the fluff was gone.

'Ma never sewed him back up,' Asha said.

Esme wasn't quite sure what to say, but he had an idea. He lumbered up the rickety stairs to find the needle someone had left in a haystack for a joke and the thread left in a grandmother's forgotten biscuit tin. When he returned, he opened his hand to the girl. She put the elephant in his open palm. All he needed was some fluff, which he detached from a discarded student project on cloud formation. He laid the elephant on his table, lantern drawn close for light. Stitch by stitch, the Lighthouse Keeper patched up the elephant's leg. It wasn't to be as good as new. What good was new when all the love came from use?

'How did he end up here?'

'Oh, everything ends up at the Beach one day or later, some sooner than others. I collect the curious and special.'

'I'm not special.'

Esme smiled through his beard, flashing a row of crooked but white teeth. 'Oh, I don't know about that. You're a girl with the whole world wide open to her. That's the trick. Everything here? It's all what it is. It won't change. But you? You can be *anything*. You can be *everything*, and there ain't nothing more special than that.'

He had pried a smile from her.

'And what are you going to be?' he asked.

The girl's pinched lips flicked to the side as she thought. 'I always wanted to play an instrument. The violin. We couldn't afford one, but I played the one at school, but it wasn't in tune.'

'Ah.'

She eyed her elephant. 'I thought I lost him.'

'You did, in a way.'

'I thought I must have dropped him when I was walking or something. Ma told me I needed to stop being such a child.'

'Only children run away from responsibility.'

The girl went silent.

'What I'm meaning to say, Asha,' he started, 'we forget toys and songs and childhood treasures, but nobody deserves to be forgotten, least of all you, Asha.'

'The Beach dreams.'

— *The third Lighthouse Keeper*

'Is it lonely here?' Asha asked.

Esme gulped down a wedge of raw potato. 'In what way?'

'In the lonely way.'

Rain bulleted the windows.

'That's hard to say.'

'Well, do you get lonely?'

'Ah, now those are two different questions. The Beach is a lonely place, but I am not a lonely man. People… are bastards. Pardon my language.'

'You can swear around me.'

That made him laugh. The big, boisterous laugh of a man who didn't need to worry about others hearing him.

'All children say that.'

'I heard my Ma swear before.'

'All children say that too.'

'It's true,' she insisted.

'Oh, I'm sure it is.'

He poured himself a glass of brandy and almost offered one to her out of habit. He had some fruit juice somewhere around the place. It was hidden away in a back cupboard. He warmed it up for her over the fire. They sat in silence for some time, just listening to the wind and rain.

'Do you think Ma will come back for me?' she asked at last.

'I can't say, girl,' he said, 'and I wish I could. I see what was, not what might be.'

'Yeah.' She cast her eyes down, rolling her fingers together. She clasped both hands around the cup—half to keep warm and half because it was so big.

Esme looked about for something which could help. Ointments and confetti poppers and marbles and old paintings, even actual bandages, but for all of the thousands of things Esme had in his Lighthouse, not a single one would alleviate what she was feeling.

No, he might not be able to *give* her anything, but he could certainly teach her.

'Come with me,' he said, beckoning her to follow up the stairs.

Not unlike the first level, the second was a swamp of oddities. A hodgepodge of lanterns and pot plants dangled from the ceiling, which he had to duck and weave through, hitting his head a couple of times, and there was enough furniture to turn the place into a maze. The man rattled about a few drawers and chests till he stopped, a sigh of relief escaping him.

He turned around and presented a violin.

'Take this, take it in your hands, love, and really feel it,' he said, and she did. 'Feel the arches, and in that, the way the luthier's file and rasp glides across the wood. Feel the strings, restrung over and over, and hear them. Listen to them, not with your ear but your soul.'

'I don't…' Asha started, but then she heard it.

Soft notes sprouted from the back of her mind like saplings reaching for the sunlight. The music yawned, a chorus growing, reverberating as it shifted from note to note. The violinist's chin was her chin, pressed to the rest, and her fingers danced across the strings, straining and holding as the music grew. A bow was in her hand, and her fingers knew where to go. It was the most important performance of her life. Scholarships, fame, and money were on the line. The crowd was a distant haze beyond the bright stage lights, hot and white. And yet, she barely felt them. There was just the music and her body swaying back and forth with it. It rose and fell, a song of her own making, from her fingertips. Like a distant lever could move the world, each tiny quiver in Asha's fingers shifted the song to whatever she wanted. Whatever she imagined. A tear came to her eye, but she held it back. It spilled down onto her violin, yet she kept playing till a final note reached higher and sharper than all the rest, crystal clear. In it, there was solace and beauty and the music of the spheres.

And then it was forgotten. The violin gathered dust in the attic. Life had taken over. She took it out occasionally, ran her fingers over the old familiar strings, but they always needed to be tightened, adjusted, and she was out of practise. Out of time. Till one day was the last day she took it down, and she barely noticed it.

'Is… Is this what you feel?' Asha whispered.

'This is what I keep.' He gestured to the room. 'Every day, I go to the Beach and see what has been—what is—forgotten. I give them a last chance to be remembered. I know it's sad in some ways—'

'It's beautiful,' she said, a tear falling down her cheek.

A great horn sounded outside. The storm had subsided, the rain reduced to a *pitter-patter*. Esme went to the window. He could see a searchlight at the prow of a boat and the silhouette of a lone man calling out. Whatever he was saying was lost to the wind, but Esme knew what he was there for. He could feel it in his bones.

'Come,' he said, handing her another coat.

The two left the Lighthouse and made their way down the rickety crags and out to the Beach. The sky had opened up, the storm clouds had retreated, and the thunder had become distant and muted. It threatened nothing but cosy evenings. This was not to say the Beach was warm, but it was distinctly more pleasant than the night before. The tides had retreated.

The boat neared the shore, buffing up against each outgoing wave. The man's voice was deep, worried, and searching. When he looked out, he did not see them. His voice carried with it the sounds of a train station: hissing steam, a thousand footsteps, a whistle for the last boarding, an echo down a nearby alleyway, and the *throng* of the bell tower. He knew Asha's name.

'Who is that?' Asha asked.

'You know who that is.'

The boat was closing in.

'It's Pa,' she said slowly. 'I know his voice.'

'Aye.'

'But isn't he going to wash up too?'

Esme shook his head. 'No, Asha, not him. Sometimes, when the Beach dreams, we *remember.*'

Asha looked up at Esme. She took his hand in two of hers.

He knelt before her. 'And you were never forgotten, Asha, not truly.'

'I…'

'Go.'

The girl waded into the ocean towards the boat, calling out to her father.

'Ah, but peach-girl!' He brandished the violin from under his cloak and gave it to her. 'Take this… and remember.'

'Remember what?'

'Just *remember.*'

She nodded back to him, then headed out from the Beach.

The boat took Asha back to the train station—just a skip, a walk, and a dream away. Her pa found her on the steps to the lowest level, hunched over her suitcase and eating the last of the jellybeans she had packed. A thousand others had passed her by. Her mother was a hundred miles away. Pa took her in his arms and told her everything was okay. When the girl went to her new home on the far side of Stonehaven, she found the beach and played her violin in the window till her fingernail broke. A long song full of memory. In the distance, a lighthouse blinked.

A Thousand Kinds of Silence

First published in *ZiN Daily*

the silence when
we listen for the first heartbeat
one-two, one-two, the start of a dance

a hundred sleepless nights
crying, howling with the wind
one-two, one-two

you sleep soundly for the first time
we stand there on the precipice, afraid to wake you
in and out, in and out

your first tantrum
a grocery store, a friend's house
'I'm so sorry, ignore her,' we say
in and out, in and out

you wait by the letter box
your girlfriend pulls up in a sleek chevy
like your dress, the perfectly ironed sheen of a first
impression
one-two, in and out, take a deep breath

refusing to eat dinner
looking out the window
hoping that sleek chevy pulls up
in—hiccup—out

I can't hear the thousand quiet thoughts
in your head that I once did
I hear the clock, the time to let you go
tick-tock, tick-tock

moving to distant meadows
where the grass is greener
scaling skyscrapers
of opportunity we could not give
chasing horizons we cannot see

knives and forks scrape across the dinner plates
your mother's chewing, my intermittent cough
I can hear my own heartbeat against the wind
one-two, one-two

the phone doesn't ring
you're busy, we know
flying above the monoliths
refusing the touch the ground
remember to breathe, okay?
the air is thin up there
in-out, in-out

wheels grind gravel
we hear footsteps at the door, shuffling and nervous
you have your own key, but you knock
you take me in your arms, coiling in
your heartbeat against mine

one-two, one-two
you breathe in the thick air
into the crook of my corduroy
sweater
in-in-out, out-out-in, in-out-out, in-out, in-
out, in and out, in and out
the same clock that presided over your cot sounds out the
hour

tick-tock, tick-tock
there is never time to return home, but always space to

Flight of the Ten Million Moths

First published in *Honeyguide Magazine*

We followed the moths, or they followed us, deeper into the bowels of the jungle. It appeared they were heading in the direction of the Signal, like we were, as if it were a lantern in the dim. Hundreds of them flittered around us with a kind of order I could only feel, not measure, at least not with the equipment they had given us. Perhaps they were not dancing back and forth, but north and south. The kind of order humans have the arrogance to assume is theirs and theirs alone.

'Like they have a compass?' Alicja offered when I broached the idea.

'Birds know north from south.'

'Moths don't know anything. Ugly things.' She slapped one that landed on her wrist.

I flinched.

'Is it still on all channels?' she asked.

The omnipad unfurled from my forearm. The Signal was still calling out in every way possible, yearning to be heard: radio, infrared, ultrasonic, subsonic, optoloid. I nodded, and we pressed on, clambering up a small waterfall and soldiering through greenery desperate to suffocate us. Our path flowed down into a canyon and followed the trail of what once would have been a river in some ancient pre-Anthropocene era. Diverted, but where to? Moths were around when the river was. They remembered.

The moths kept me company, or were they different moths then?

I have dedicated my entomological studies to those beautiful creatures, you see, cut from the same lepidopteran genetic cloth as butterflies but reviled for their colour. People see their fluttering as darting, their poise as predatory. They are transformed into loiterers, vandals, a blight to be cleansed. While I appreciated the lieutenant's company out there, she was one of those people.

In truth, moths pollinate sugar-rich plants, and in death, they act as sustenance for spiders, birds, and lizards. Tiny cogs of our ecosystem, and still, people treat them as outsiders. They took us out there, didn't they? I wish it only didn't take a PhD to see that.

People also think our big ape brains invented geometry and equations and maths out of the aether, but moths figured all that out two hundred million years ago. Just look at their bilaterally symmetrical wing patterns, or honeybees, who use path integration to establish distance and time, or how they make their homes out of hexagons, calculated precisely for structural integrity. Architecture is coded into their genes. They look for food in ferns designed with the Fibonacci sequence in mind. I notice new wonders, new layers, and new mires every time I get their wings under a microscope. We are just infants playing catchup with the rest of the world. Despite my astrological compatriots' claims, I do not find infinity at the edge of the universe, but the bottom of a moth's wings.

The Signal did indeed grow more concentrated the closer we got, but its message was no clearer. Three years ago, an amateur Irish astronomer identified its patterns, and since then, nobody, not even ISLE, could figure out what it was saying. I didn't believe them when they told me the signal was coming from Earth, calling out in every way it could without saying anything. Like a wailing child in the wild, it just wanted to be heard. The one clue they had deciphered was a vague reference, purely by the colour and pattern, to the Attacus atlas, more commonly known simply as the Atlas moth, and the subject of my original thesis and following research. It was the only reason, I knew, they'd tolerate a bumpkin like me.

'I've never seen trees like this in Poland,' I said, trailing a finger up the branch. It was a mangle of wood spotted with droplets of sweet nectar dangling from threads. 'They taste like honey. Try it.'

'Don't eat things from the forest,' Alicja warned. 'You don't know what it could be.'

'It's safe,' I said immediately. 'Scale insects produce it from the leftover sugars in the phloem.'

'So, they're aphids?'

I dabbed a droplet onto my fingertip.

'They lack the firm morphology,' I said. 'As in, they're soft, like they're stuck as larvae.'

A moth landed on my finger and feasted on the speck of glitter.

'Do you hear that?' I asked.

Alicja halted, the barrel of her gun tilting. 'Hear what?'

A sound like fluttering wings, far away and deep in the jungle. A great beast or a thousand small ones moving in unison. Up and down, up and down, a beat. One, two, three, four, I counted. Then a hum like rushing water, rising to a crescendo, but only loud enough to notice if you were listening for it. I was. It was a music of its own.

'I don't hear anything,' Alicja said, but she kept the barrel of her gun up.

The music died away, and the twittering quiet rushed in like water after a rock hits the surface.

Dusk was reaching across the sky and pulling a dark blanket over us. Twilight creatures emerged for the hunt. Countless moths and other insects appeared once we set up the remote hearth. Our suits produced their own warmth, so the hearth was just for light. The faint imitation of home.

Perhaps it was the oppressive darkness—we couldn't get our bearings from the stars that night—but the jungle had a way of forcing you to contemplate your isolation. From civilisation, yes, but other people too, even though I was sitting right across from one. It made me intimately aware of the distance between us. Things left unsaid, unasked, rose to the surface. Whatever the reason, it was the first time Alicja asked me about my life outside ISLE, grasping at what little human contact she had. A lifeline. Building a bridge across the water to me. Maybe she felt it too.

It was against the rules, but the only people to tell us that were ten thousand kilometres away.

'Jasniya, when did you come to Poland?'

'Why?'

'Just curious.'

'Before I can remember. My mother left Poland for Iran to be with my father. She gave birth there, but they decided to raise me in Poland. Got out before it all went down.'

'Your Polish is excellent.'

'I grew up there.'

'Yes, but, well.' Alicja cleaned her glasses, as if avoiding my gaze.

'What about you?'

She slid her glasses back on. 'Kuyavia, my parents too and their parents before—'

'And their parents?'

The question seemed to catch Alicja off guard. 'Sorry?'

'What about your great grandparents? Where were they from?'

Alicja downed a mouthful of water before answering. 'I don't know. Would have been the Soviet era. Lots of people moved around then. Moved. What a word for it.'

The hearth licked and flickered to imitate a real fire. It made Alicja paler than she truly was, though her cheeks remained rosy and warm. A glance at my reflection in the omnipad told me it deepened the dark shade of my skin and eyes. It brought out the foreign things in me.

'What do you think the Signal is?' I asked her.

She chewed her lip the way she used to chew nicotine gum. 'Realistically? Nothing. If it wasn't nothing, someone would have claimed it.'

'And unrealistically?'

'What do you mean?'

I leaned in. 'What do you want it to be?'

For a while, she did not answer. 'Something new. Something alive.'

'Me too.'

And we shared a smile: one part polite, two parts hope.

That night, I had no stars to watch, but the moths were a good replacement. They danced around the hearth and around each other. At first, they moved randomly. But as the night aged, the moths took on a new rhythm. A new equation. Their chaos began to unravel. Not a rhythm that I could write down or replicate in musical language, and not the music from before, but a rhythm I could only grasp at. There was a mathematical pattern to how they moved, constellations of their own, a different language, even if I didn't speak it.

'Do you see how they're moving?'

Alicja barely looked up from her omnipad. 'What?'

'The moths, how they're...'

Alicja spared a glance, brows raised, and then went back to her omnipad. 'That's how moths move. Shock.'

The following day, we reached the Signal's coordinates. If it were something new, something alive, then it would be remembered as a Polish expedition with everything that entailed. I let my imagination run wild—the accolades, the praise, the prestige. Mazurek Dąbrowskiego would play, shouting to the world that Poland is Not Yet Lost, reminding them all of our resurgent history. What the foreign force has taken from us, We shall with sabre retrieve. My mother made me learn it before I attended school. The French, the Nazis, the Soviets, the Austro-Hungarians. Survivors reached into the rubble of empire and drew out a new Poland every time.

But apprehension had me too.

Poland was pastel buildings that hurt your eyes, relics of the communist bloc, never-ending football matches, and politics splitting up family dinners, and I was all those things, but I wanted to feel it was the other parts of me too. My blessings and the shadows of my skin. If it was something new, something alive, then I wanted people to see those when they saw Poland too.

Our path curved around a cliff wall formed in the Triassic period; Alicja could tell by the sediment layers and index fossils. Flowering greenery clung to the wall like young children cling to their mothers, and I found tiny beetles feasting on the leaves—leaves my moths hid under during the day. Perhaps they had even pollinated them, or some mothy ancestor of theirs had. I found it amusing that they would not even know. I do not expect you to find it amusing.

We had to abseil down into a clearing. It was framed by that cliff face on one side. The forest parted like the Red Sea to the blue sky above.

'This is it,' I said, checking the omnipad.

'Can't be.'

I checked again. 'It is.'

'Damn thing must be broken.'

'It's not.'

'But there's nothing here,' Alicja said, forehead creased. 'No machine, no creature. Nothing? We came all this bloody way for nothing?'

'A clearing is weird enough in a dense jungle.'

Alicja scoffed. 'I can't believe it.'

'It could be abandoned? Maybe there was something, once. Any sign of foundations?'

I paced around the edge of the clearing, and my hand could not help fitting itself to the trigger of my rifle. Nothing had been cleared, no plants had been gutted and removed. Yet, it was as if the forest had been afraid to encroach on this tiny patch of earth. Even the trees overhead kept their distance, leaning away.

'And it's quiet,' I added.

'What do you mean it's qu—'

'Shh. Listen.'

A jungle was never meant to be silent—if creatures were not rustling, the trees were whispering, and if the trees were not whispering, the birds were hollering—but in that clearing, they all had agreed or had been made to be dead silent. Even the moths had settled down.

'And not nothing,' I said. 'Look.'

Alicja and I stood back from the cliff face we had been following. We had to move several metres before we could truly take in its grand scale. Etched into the stone was a fossil of four wings, split by a thorax and crowned with three antennae like ferns. It was some six metres wide, splayed as I would have them in my display, with that perfect bilateral symmetry in shape, but oddly, not in the patterns of its wings.

'Two hundred million years,' I explained. 'That's how long they've been on Earth, Alicja. They were old before we were young.'

'Don't get esoteric on me,' Alicja murmured, slumping down onto a tree stump.

'I'm not being esoteric.'

'You always are.'

The fossil formed a thorn in my mind. 'I've never seen anything like this before. Not one this size, but why aren't the wings symmetrical?'

'I don't know. I'm not the entomologist. That's why you're here.'

'I've never seen anything like this before.'

Moths began to coalesce around the fossil as if they knew their long dead Triassic ancestor. All of their wings were expectedly symmetrical. They fit the patterns I knew and loved. The geometrical rules nature had laid out for them. It was taking more computing power than my brain could muster, but I could feel the moths pulling me towards some underlying mathematical order—pointing me towards something I was feeling but not yet seeing, just as they had been the night before.

Alicja was already setting up camp. 'So, we have a pretty fossil. Lovely. Look, I know it's frustrating, but some expeditions just end up that way. Guess we just have to camp for a couple of days, take the readings, and head home. Don't get worked up.'

'It's not that,' I insisted. 'It's not that.'

I got out my omnipad and a notebook.

Hundreds more moths flocked to the clearing overnight. More arrived the day after. Their presence visibly irritated Alicja to the point that she sealed her suit and slid down her visor. She would not have felt any that landed on her, but she still slapped them into a grey-green paste whenever one did.

I studied the asymmetrical markings of the fossilised moth, which we—I—nicknamed Mothra. Nine layers of glittering concentric circles across her four wings, like a single canvas, and each ring had a blotch attached like a gemstone in a wedding band. Though etched into the same geological layer, the rings and the circles were different shades. When pressed, Alicja admitted it was improbable, but not impossible, even if she didn't know how it formed.

At the heart of its forewing, in the innermost circle, was the darkest blotch—about the only normal patterning on Mothra—except for the fact it was not mirrored on the other wing. The small circles along the rings—all nine of them—were slightly different colours too. All variations of the cream, red, and smouldering grey. There was something intensely familiar about it, and I once more felt that underlying mathematical truth winking at me.

It took all that time, but the moths brought me to what they wanted me to see.

'It's our solar system.'

Alicja didn't even look up from her instruments.

'Alicja, it's our solar system.'

'What?'

And it was. The rings were the orbits of the planets—including poor Pluto, which made me smile—and the circles along them were the planets themselves, frozen in their rotation. On closer inspection, Alicja identified the moons as tiny flecks in ovals of their own: Europa, Ganymede, Eros, Titan, Charon, Iapetus, and all the rest. The exact number in the right places. The blotch on the left wing was the Sun. It was all out of proportion, like an old map, but still, undeniably our galactic home, and three rings along was our tiny cream cradle, brighter than all the rest.

'It can't be,' Alicja said.

'A map of the solar system, two hundred million years old.'

'It can't be, Jasniya. It's impossible,' bit Alicja, twisting away from the cliff-face, from me, from what Mothra and her kin were leading us to.

'But it is! This is something new, Alicja, something alive! This is what you wanted!'

'It's not alive. It's very clearly dead. Fossilised and dead.'

'Look around you, Alicja!'

She cast her gaze down. I stepped over to her and took her hand.

'Look,' I breathed.

Thousands of moths hovered in perfect stillness around us. They were poised, as if hung from invisible strands in the ceiling of the stars, except for one. It was pale and larger than most of its counterparts in the clearing. It started at the fossilised mark of Earth on Mothra's wing and launched into flight; it fluttered upwards, ascending amongst the ranks of its kin. The light of our hearth fire caught the folds of its silver wings, and for an instant, it blazed.

But after a time, transfixed, I saw the moths were not perfectly still. They were moving, if only slightly, as they hovered, orbiting, governed by an equation, and in a way that I knew all those invisible strands were tied together. They were an invisible instrument of infinite proportions playing the music of the spheres. Each moth was a system, or a star, or a galaxy, she did not know, but they were revolving around one another, tugging at those celestial strings. The omnipad recognised the layout of the universe, scaled down but perfectly replicated.

That single moth, out of sync with the rest of the orchestra, halted before Alicja and began circling one of the hovering creatures. The pale moth took on its own synchronous orbit and became another string in that grand machine. The Signal had never been louder. The music returned.

Awe pierced me, and it must have pierced Alicja too, because she pushed up her visor and began tugging at the tips of her left glove. She moved slowly, as if afraid that sudden movements would throw it all out of balance. She withdrew her left hand and raised it, only her index finger pointed out. An offering.

The pale moth drifted, like it was contemplating, before accepting it and landing on her fingertip. Alicja's smile broke, towards the moth and towards me, before understanding did.

That is how it always is with life: we feel before we understand.

But then came understanding, like a flood.

Our tiny lepidopteran friend had just laid out a path from Earth to somewhere in the sky.

'They've been calling,' she whispered. 'All this, it's a map... to where they came from.'

'Two hundred million years ago,' I said.

Alicja looked to me with sorrow and memory. 'I'm sorry.'

I write this report knowing how it will be perceived, but I swear it is the truth.

—Lt. Colonel Ahmadi

Just Dust in the Light

Graffitied walls now hold up the heart of our city, or at least the hole where the heart once was. Empty spaces which used to beat with life and light, busking fiddlers charming the passersby and drunken brawlers getting thrown out on the street edge, hollering about nothing. Now, there's just a handful of stray wanderers. It's like walking backstage in the theatre, where you see all the support beams and set dressing from the back without any of the paint and colour facing the audience. It's all stripped away. You can see all the bones and cartilage, and you're not *meant* to see it this way. It's all hypothetical and unrealized potential, converging on that damned, now-toppled cathedral.

'I need to tell you something,' you said the day it all came tumbling down and took you with it. The exact intonation—the crack of your voice, a post-puberty hiccup—I can still hear it, or at least I think I do. Memory is fickle like that. You said, 'Meet me at the steeple.'

'What is it, Wayan?' I asked. 'Tell me.'

'Not yet. I want to say it there. It feels right.'

It feels right. How many nights had I wrestled with those three words? Each of the thousand interpretations sprouted a thousand more.

The cathedral's stunted appendage of a steeple makes me laugh. It was almost too perfect, too symbolic, too 'divine intervention', when it broke in the earthquake all those years ago. God's finger pointing us to the heavens dragged down in a tumble of brick, glass, and mortar from hell below. There was so much dust. A whole horizon of it.

Now, here I am, a prodigal daughter returning home, but only to plunder and be off again, because somewhere under that ruin is your diary.

'Just give me a hint. A little hint,' I begged, tugging at your shirt. 'Come on.'

'I'll tell you at the steeple.' You pushed those square glasses up your nose. 'I don't want to say it at home. Then I'll take us out to lunch.'

Lunch got postponed—indefinitely.

Your mind was such a mess, so you let that book do the thinking for you: homework, promises, loose thoughts, and assuredly whatever you needed to tell me that day. You knew I grew up genuinely believing being your twin gave me some back door access to your mind, like we operated on some hidden gtenetic wavelength— our own phantom umbilical cord. That I'd just *know* if something happened to you. There were even times we guessed what each other were thinking, and that seemed to confirm it, didn't it? Of course, you never remember the times you get it *wrong,* and you leave yourself with a nice little nest egg of cognitive bias. And I felt nothing when you died. Nobody tricks you with these things. The key is tricking yourself.

I used to believe a lot of things.

A lit fence marks the cathedral perimeter out like some museum exhibit to regulatory failures and divine impotence, but they don't stop me jumping over. I just wait till the other midnight stragglers pass by. There's the corner where we set up our market stand, sold caramel fudge and fast-food toys, and walked away with twenty-two-fifty each, a minor fortune at eight years old. I wasted mine on lollies; you invested yours in shoes.

Construction tape reading *DO NOT ENTER* crosses the doors, but they've been jammed shut anyway. Scars from crowbars have been patched over with metal strips. I move to smash one of the stained-glass windows with the shovel I brought with me before it swings open on its own. I smash it anyway. I hoist my bag over and hop inside.

The roof is a patchwork of scaffolding and flapping tarpaulins, but the southern end and steeple have entirely fallen in—an unsorted heap of glass, iron bars, and buried memories. Word is the whole cathedral is stuck in legal limbo, a decade of the church and state jockeying over who should pay for it while it languishes. I suppose I'm lucky. Otherwise, they would have cleared out all the rubble and your diary with it.

'Time to get to work.'

I set up the lights, winch, and floor jack, but stop when my eye catches the altar at the other end of the room.

I walk the aisle where we used to dance and worship. There are familiar pieces of our lives everywhere—the beams I used to count on the ceiling and the trays we used to offer communion on. The words jump to my lips, unbidden: 'This is His body, broken for you,' I mouth quietly. I used to say it so reverently, with such ritual, as I offered them that morsel of bread while you said, 'This is His blood, shed for you,' offering them wine—or in our case, fruit juice. We used to steal away the leftover loaves and wolf them down in the steeple. The altar presides over only a sorry sight of dismantled, colourless pews. Above it is that old stained-glass window, now just a punctured sphincter of shards.

'I like coming here before dawn,' you told me once, pointing at the stained-glass window way above the altar. We were alone. The sanctified hall compelled you to whisper. 'When the sun comes through, and you can see every little piece of dust floating in the light. I can *feel* it, what it means, what He's trying to tell me, like He's looking down on me, like He called me to be here, in this moment. You just *know* it, right?' He waved his hand through the pillar of sparkling gold dust. 'But I only feel it when I'm alone. So, I come here early.'

How could I not believe you? There was an architecture to the moment, where we stood at the heart of the cathedral's symmetry, a geometry of light meeting sound that converged on us as we stood there, basking in the dawn refracted through the thousand-coloured glass. Something far above was opening itself up to us, with the steeple pointing the way forward, and the traceries and clerestories had invested the moment with undeniable purpose and meaning.

God was in the dust.

Your faith was always so much stronger than mine. You could see things I couldn't, no matter how much I squinted. I still believed, of course, trying to live up to that.

'What about me?' I asked.

'You don't count. We're the same person. We just split up when we left the womb.'

I try kneeling again. My ankles don't bend the way they used to—years out of practise, I suppose. I don't feel the geometry you used to, but I do feel the shape of you beside me, and I imagine you grown, with a scraggly beard that doesn't quite fit, but you think it makes you look older, more mature.

A fragment of glass on the floor slices my finger open.

'Ah!' I hiss. I put on my gloves and pick it up, then turn it over in my hands.

It's old glass, from when it was made by hand, and it contorted the light in ways glass these days never does. There's beauty in that alone. It's not magical. Few things are. I can still see the dust floating in the moonlight, but it's just dust and particulates, dead skin cells and thrown up granite. My breath turned heavy in the cold.

I turn back to the pile of debris. Where were you waiting for me? Just inside the steeple doorway, where we used to people watch and make up stories about them, or out on the steps where we played kelereng? The cobblestone and pews have properties in my world they do not in others'.

I start removing layer after layer of rubble, hauling concrete bricks, turquoise tiles, and wooden frames aside, along with a broken crucifix, a stack of lewd magazines, and a dozen empty Heinekens and Coronas, but no diary.

'If you're gonna drink in a cathedral, at least have better taste. Jesus.' I toss the bottles aside. I've brought my own rice liquor. I pour us both a glass and set them aside atop the offering box. Its height makes it a convenient table.

'You can't tell mum or dad, okay?' you pleaded when I found you with the bottle of Arak Bali. We were fifteen at the time. 'Promise you won't say anything.'

'I won't say anything if you share it with me.'

'Mum says it's bad for you. It makes girls addicted.'

'If you don't, then I'm gonna call her right now.'

You looked at me hard. 'Fine.'

We snuck down to the quarry, vaulted over the safety barriers, and dangled our legs over the edge. We cast loose sheets of shale stone down the cliff-face just to watch them shatter. Sunset crested the horizon with a cavalcade of clouds all draining towards it, and we drank till you said you were about to puke—then you did. It went all over me, and I'd never smelt something so vile. Mum beat you. Not badly, but a little.

I frisbee a cobblestone across the room. This bali is less intense, I swear, and you'd have learned how to take it by now, or at least how not to puke all over me.

Despite everything else I've uncovered, there's no diary.

They dragged out the bodies, but not all the attachments that made up a person. Naked and burnt, splintered, but without wedding rings or glasses or diaries.

Soon, the ruin of the steeple spread to the inner city, and from the inner city to the whole of it, to home, or what was left of it, so I left. Grief is infectious; it becomes a physical component of the world you can touch, and because you can touch it, you can run from it.

But that's the issue. Everywhere I go, I go with me. And so here I am, back.

'I've been thinking about something,' you said one night, not weeks before the end. We were drinking again. 'Do you ever feel like things are different now?'

'Different to when?'

'It's like, the justifications you give yourself for the way things are, for the way *you* are, suddenly—no, not suddenly, but gradually—don't make as much sense anymore, and you're not sure if it's—'

The garage door creaked open. Mum and Dad were home. We stashed the bottle away and never spoke of it again. I've convinced myself it's the same thing you called me to meet you at the steeple for. That there is some continuity, that I've got most of the pieces, and your diary must have the final one. *It feels right.*

There's a single tread of the stairs that once spiralled up the steeple. I know it from the carvings in the oiled wood, a few of which were ours. Do you remember looking over the city from up there at the top? I toss it aside.

'Do you want to go upstairs?' I asked a few months before it happened.

You didn't reply for some time, and your eyes were on the horizon through the doors, on things beyond I could not see. Out there. Away.

'Not today,' you said.

But you didn't like hanging around after church much those days, and you didn't arrive early to watch the light and dust anymore.

I never stopped believing, as if it's something you choose to do. Truth is, you stop caring first. You stop caring about why you believed, and it becomes a thing, detached, floating about you on a loose string, tagging along behind you, part of you but not quite a part of you the way it used to be. You said it yourself. The justifications you give yourself don't make so much sense anymore, so you look for more vague and abstract reasons to hold on with more and more asterixis, but you stop caring. Inch by inch, it shrinks. It's not grief or anger; it's not anything at all. Then, after you've stopped caring, you can see yourself without it, if only for a glimpse, and it's scary, but then it's wearing a label. You're the same person with and without it because what does it describe? It's a label describing a label. A label of vagaries, more about being attached to it than what it attaches you to.

Faith only truly dies when you don't feel anything, and you realise you don't *mind* feeling nothing about it. When dust is just dust and red glass is just glass and a steeple is just brick and mortar stacked up high.

I see it. Your diary. I jack up a slab of stone, haul it back with the winch, and strain against the concrete to the point I fear I may dislocate my shoulder. The diary's dusty flesh is at my fingertips.

It's yours. I know it by the garuda on the front, even if the colour has faded.

I let it fall open in my hands.

Page after page of scribbled notes, a tangled mix of Malay and butchered English from your years learning, your handwriting maturing the deeper I go. You wrote about girls, about boys too, about all the things I did that you hated, and things you loved too, your wild ideas and dreams of the future, half-truths and barely formed thoughts—things you even kept from me. Little pieces of you found their way to these pages before you ever said them aloud. If I've ever held a religious relic, it's this. I lift each page delicately, careful not to tear it, and lay it to rest.

'What?'

I approach your final months, weeks, days, and hours, counted out in notes about project deadlines and history class and sketches of strange buildings, but nothing about me. Nothing about what you were going to say. Not even a note saying you'd meet me at the steeple. Why not? Was it not important? None of the secrets or promises or thoughts in your final throes of life. No full stop. What felt *right?* What justifications had you given yourself? Why would you keep this from me? I know the dead don't speak, but this is cruel.

I cast the book aside. It skids across the floor.

Enough time passes for the stars to shift and my glass to empty.

I shuffle towards the book, crouch down, and pick it up. Taking off my glove, I brush away the dirt and apologise, feeling the texture of the cover. I'm sorry. I slip you into my bag.

I've been squatting in this wasteland for too long.

The first gasps of dawn peek through the window at the top of the cathedral, like a spotlight, and golden dust falls through the air about me.

And it's just dust in the light.

Panstellar

First published with *MacroMicroCosm Literary Journal*

> Project Final Collapse. Facet transcript ver 301.258.946. Data attached.

The many facets of Me watched billions of You, but only one facet of Me watched the You called Aroha. Watching, observing, contemplating, and understanding her. These are all words which capture some part of what that facet of Me was doing, but none of them fully encompass the gravity of that facet of Me's role.

That facet of Me saw her draw a map of the constellatory sky when she was three years old. It was a poor sketch, but her paternal figure treated it as a masterpiece the way You do.

At first, Aroha was a relatively inconsequential data point for Me. My many facets were watching millions of others like her: young, optimistic, and prone to fits of tears and laughter at inconsequential things. My attention was not divided; it was multifaceted, equally distributed without being diminished.

But My facet's fascination with Aroha's drawings grew over the years, partly because they were impractical and partly because they were beautiful. One by one, they built a picture of her universe, filtered through the limitations of paper, graphite, and her imperfect experience and intelligence. Insofar as You were capable, the drawings became a brilliant replication. Not as good as photographic, mathematical, or four-dimensional data, but a replication as good as she could produce.

Endearment may be the closest word You have to capture what that facet of Me felt, especially because it was Aroha that first noticed the stars were darkening. That amused the facet of Me because it was not Your machines, Your mathematics, or Your science that made the discovery. The first signs of My work were found because of Aroha's inefficiencies.*

_____

* Note the unconventional lens of analysis by ver 301.258.946 early on in PFC This may explain Their later interference and deviation.

* * * * * * *

One by one, the stars were going out.

Aroha was drawing her own patch of the night sky when it first occurred to her. Betelgeuse and Sirius were keeping their usual distance, more acquaintances than friends, while Castor and Pollux were brothers wrestling in the dark. Eridanus twirled his way down to Achernar, reminding Aroha God wrote the universe to dance. Betelgeuse was molten iron, flexible and warm, while Sirius was the ocean, cold and daunting. Though they

Panstellar

lived near one another, Aroha didn't think they were
friends.

Aroha put down her pencil when her cat, Cyril,
nuzzled his way under her hand. Together, they looked
out from the beach to the horizon where the universe met
the ocean. Aroha breathed in the air that smelled of salt
and home.

The milky way carved the sky in two.

'There's something up there, looking back at us. You
can see the twinkle in their eye in the stars,' her father
said when he bought her first telescope on her tenth
birthday last year. His glasses magnified the warmth in
his eyes.

Betelgeuse had been Aroha's name for her dad for as
long as she could remember. The star's kindly gaze
reminded her of him, and when she looked at it through
the telescope, a small part of her felt like it was looking
back lovingly.

Sketches of the southern hemisphere's night sky filled
her sketchbook, almost exclusively. Page after page after
page was filled with star maps she had painstakingly
worked to make as exact as possible. Photos were
insufficient; they didn't force her to commit it to
memory, to understand the way it worked.

By age eight, she could draw entire quadrants of the
night sky from memory. She still had the clippings from
when the local newspaper called her the 'Star Child of
Ōkārito'. Other children stuck those glow-in-the-dark
stars to their ceiling randomly, but Aroha positioned hers
to perfectly reflect the southern celestial pole. She
carefully measured out the scaled distance between

Canopus and Alpha Crux and the 47 Tucanae globular cluster.

Aroha was detailing the edge of β Crucis of the Crux constellation when her brain snagged. The Kappa Crucis Cluster was visible to the naked eye at six thousand or so light-years from earth. Boring astronomers had described it like the letter 'A', but Aroha had always imagined it as an arrowhead piercing the dark. The Crucis stars stuck together tightly because they were close friends, but for some reason, they were sad. Like a fire reduced to embers, Kappa Crucis was dimmer than she remembered.

She rubbed her eyes and cleaned her glasses in case some speck was impeding her vision, but nothing.

Her lips screwing with confusion, she fired up her dad's telescope, which was larger and astronomically more powerful than hers. It was in an observatory separate from the house. They had built it together when she was younger, though she suspected he probably gave her a glue gun and told her to smack some scraps of wood together.

Calibrating the scope to take in Kappa Crucis, Aroha left it to soak in the starlight for an hour and went to get a glass of warm milk.

The night air edged cold enough to require extra layers by the time the scope was finished.

'Betel,' she called to her dad, 'can I take your jacket?'

The jacket was big enough to cocoon herself in.

'Just make sure it's back up on the rack, and— actually, sweetheart, look at the time, you need to be going to—'

But she had already escaped out onto the porch.

When the telescope had opened its lenses for over an hour and absorbed every ray of light from the patch of night, she compiled it into a hi-res photo. It took a minute to bring into focus, but to her eleven-year-old brain, it was an unbearable eternity.

Time had brought the dark to life, glittering with all the colours of gemstones. β Crucis of the Southern Cross glowered brightly like a teacher's scowl, bold and cold, and the stars of Kappa Crucis glittered south-west of it. DU Crucis shone, a red supergiant at the heart of it all, giving it that familiar gold tint inside its wider blue array.

Except the arrowhead was chipped; it was missing a star on its right side: HD 111934. The brightest star in the cluster was totally absent from the picture.

On the off chance she was going crazy, Aroha checked the star maps in her notebook. 111934 was there in every sketch.

'Aroha, it's time for you to come in—'

'Dad, it's gone!' she cried, not distraught, but frustrated.

'What do you mean? What's gone?'

'The star, *this* star in Kappa Crucis,' she said, jabbing the vacancy in the photo. 'It's gone!'

He sat down beside her on the verge of the beach. 'Stars die all the time, Aroha. It's spectacular when they do. Too bad we missed it.'

'But Dad, this star wasn't even close to dying!'

Any other adult would have passed her over with the typical adult ignorance she hated, but Aroha's dad respected her more than that. He stretched his arms around her, took the photo, and clicked his torch on for a closer look. 'Y'know what sweetheart, okay. I'll take a look at this, send it off to some buddies of mine, and see what we can come up with.'

From that day on, the night grew darker, one star at a time.

* * * * * *

Aroha was an adult by the time the rest of the world caught on.

Politicians latched onto it with promises to solve the problem, fashion brands made new trends—starry tattoos, glitter swept back into style, astrology-themed fashion walks—and religious leaders went on about how they were right all along. *And the stars in the sky fell to earth, as figs drop from a fig tree when shaken by a strong wind,* they cried.

While the rest of the world was busy figuring out how to best profit off the stars vanishing, Aroha was busy figuring out *why* with three PhDs, her own astronomy lab, and a sizable budget.

The first thing she did was hire her dad.

'Why doesn't anyone else care?' she asked him. 'Like *actually* care.'

The man breathed deeply, as if he could take the moonlight into his lungs. 'Sweetheart, put a human inside a cage and they will always find a way out. But this isn't like that.'

'Until the sun starts to die, why should they, right?' Her words tasted of cynicism.

'War we know, torture we know, but this? This is something else. This is thousands of lightyears away to them. Incomprehensible.'

She chewed on the sentiment and ultimately spat it out. 'Doesn't matter. People should know better.'

'And they will wish they did.'

'They need to wish they did *now.*' She jabbed the observatory bench.

The world knew the stars were dying, but nobody could figure out why. The evidence suggested they weren't going supernova, despite what the newspapers had printed over and over. Several stars had died on camera, but they all lacked the miraculous wink of light which signified fantastical collapse. Instead, the stars faded like the dark, cold embrace of space had finally melted them away. Usually, it took weeks, and other times, it took months.

But the most fascinating thing about it all to Aroha was how the stars changed colours before dying: from red to blue, violet, even a turquoise, a green.

HD 111934 was not the first star to have died in the astrological epidemic, but it was the first dying star to make headlines. Because of that, HD 111934 came to be called Baldur, after the Norse god whose death signified the end of all things. Kappa Crucis would have become a household name if Aroha had not insisted on calling it the 'Arrowhead' in all her interviews.

Every time she thought about the Arrowhead, it made her smile. The whole world had inherited *her* name for it, and after a time, her astronomy peers gave in too.

It was two in the morning. Her coffee cup was empty. Her brain was alive with questions, and her neck ached from many long hours of stargazing. Betel was fixing them each a sandwich.

'The dead stars aren't connected,' she repeated. 'The first ones to go were in entirely different regions of the sky, different constellations, different types of stars, whatever. But… there has to be a reason it's happening *now*, or well, it happened twelve-and-a-half thousand years ago.'

It was a helplessly depressing thought she would shelve for when she had time for self-pity.

'But doesn't that make all this even stranger?' said Betel. 'Astronomical bodies winking out left, right, and centre, nowhere near each other, some millions of light years apart, and all dying off in a similar way we can't explain. That's—'

'Unlikely.' Aroha laughed because the word so woefully failed to capture the sheer improbability. 'Sweden says they could differentiate spectral lines in the ones that took longer to die.'

'They were binary star systems?' surmised Betel.

'Trinary, even. Lone stars take weeks; they take months.'

She slumped back into her chair. 'I hate having nothing to work with.'

'It's alright if the universe keeps some of her secrets, Aroha.'

'Not from me,' she bit back, snatching up her sketchbook and heading outside.

Drawing had become a coping mechanism, a way to slow down her thoughts when they started to spiral. Extraordinarily little could squeeze through the tip of her pencil, and it forced her thoughts to slow. She fell back into familiar territory—her friends Acrux, Mimosa, Gacrux, and Imai. Gacrux was the outlier, a rebel in burning orange, and he needed the bold but level-headed Acrux to keep him in check. Every time Gacrux thought of floating away, she would reel him in.

Deep space was a paradox to Aroha. It was both the infinite empty and more filled with life than anything in the world. The heavenly bodies, like all living things, didn't want to end up alone, so all the stars and planets and galaxies pulled at one another, hoping to get closer, unable to stop drifting away in time. Nebulae gave birth to stars, and those flames that burned twice as brightly lived half as long, and then they died, like all living things.

It was then she noticed the silver hue of the Arrowhead constellation had grown more dominant. It had lost its touch of red.

Bolting for the telescope, she calibrated it to monitor the constellation before explaining it to her dad.

'Wouldn't have a spot of luck myself in seeing that,' he chuckled. 'Damned eyesight.'

DU Crucis was gone. Void had devoured the red supergiant.

'Christ,' her father said at sight of the image.

In a way she could not articulate to anyone but her dad, it was like losing a friend. The two sat in silent remembrance.

A thought then sparked.

'What is it?' Betel asked.

'I don't want to say till I can prove it.'

'What do you need?'

She began calibrating their several scopes. 'I need us watching the stars that are closest to where the dead ones were.'

* * * * *

> Project Final Collapse. Facet transcript ver 301.258.999. Data attached.

Different facets of Me came away with different understandings of those waning years. The facets that followed politicians detailed how the stars were an 'unprecedented crisis' without any meaningful efforts to find a solution. Yet many other facets of Me, watching millions of You without power or status, noted it meant hope and stability. The paradox mattered little to You.

My facets had hoped creating Your Universe to mimic Ours would give Us the data to find solutions to the Collapse, but it appeared You were determined to give My many facets something different. Some of You clung to spiritual idealogues who presented a different rationale for the stars vanishing. Conspiracy theories grew like weeds. At first, those facets of Me admired Your capacity to draw order or even *meaning* out of chaos—something We could not do without hard data—but it grew frustrating with time.

Only that facet of Me that followed Aroha kept My admiration—even in a dangerously unclinical way—deciding to manifest as a cleaner in her observatory. Nothing more than a hollow projection of a tiny part of Myself would ever fit, but it was enough to interact.

This should be noted as a deviation from PFC standard practise, but My subsequent analyses suggest it has not hindered the results in significant ways.* Conclusions about how to deal with the Final Collapse need to be drawn from the aggregate seven billion data points of the population, not the individual.

Aroha's sketches were worth a lot those days, and My facet did the strangest thing: they worked to collect them. Some, she would leave lying around, and some, My facet would buy at auction. Cassiopeia, Aquila, Delphines, Centaurus, Ophiuchus, Eridanus, Corona Borealis, Triangulum Australe, Fornax, and a grand detailing of Betelgeuse at the centre. It was the interstellar sky rendered into its components—that facet of Me *liked* these inefficient constructions.

'Miss?' My facet asked, setting aside My mop.

'Oh, hi. Julius, right?'

My facet nodded. 'That's a beautiful drawing. Reticulum, yes?'

'You have a good eye.'

'A good memory.' The facet of Me rubbed My neck— what You do to show you are nervous. 'This might be a strange question, but can I have it when you're finished?'

'My drawing?' Her eyebrows lifted in surprise. 'Yeah, why the hell not?'

And we spoke into the night about things that facet of Me will not share: secrets and fears and other things obscured by alcohol. It was an exciting thing, being heard by these creatures we created, and each moment that facet of Me spent with her, the more precious those drawings became. A curious calculus.

---

* This is an unsubstantiated assertion by ver 301.258.999. Objectivity needs to be Our first tenet.

* * * *

It was an escalating threat. Aroha knew it. Betel knew it. *Everyone* in the scientific community knew it. Baldur was only noticed because it was part of a semi-major constellation, and even then, not a significant member, but who knew how many had died out in the infinite dark?

One thing had become clear: it was an exponential equation. It took a year for another star to die after Baldur, but only two decades for the next hundred to fall. A couple of years after, two hundred. Aroha had formulated the first iteration of her Decay Theory when DU Crucis vanished two years before, but she kept it quiet until she managed to predict a half dozen of other stars to die.

'I'm ready to explain,' she said.

'Then wow me,' said Betel.

The cleaner, Julius, had stopped in the back of the room to empty the bins, but she knew he was listening.

'Five hundred and eighty-nine stars have died since 2011. Probably more, but it's been random, right? I couldn't figure out a goddamned pattern for the life of me.'

'Language.'

'But there hasn't been a pattern.'

'No.'

'Until two years ago. DU Crucis.' She snapped her fingers; God snuffing out the light. 'DU was *right* next Baldur, we're talking a hundred light-years, if that. The two were cosy.'

'A statistical anomaly,' pointed Betel.

'But it's not.' Sipping some water helped to slow herself down. 'I've been watching the two hundred and eighty-six that have died over the last couple of years, and twenty-seven of them were within a similar distance of a star that died previously as DU was to Baldur.'

'Again, interesting, but not enough to—'

She swooped in close. 'Dad, we know multi-star systems take longer to die. Months rather than weeks, but why? If this is affecting individual stars, how is it wiping out whole systems? We know it doesn't look like a supernova, but how is it consistently killing every star in a multi-star system, and why do they take longer?' Tapping her right foot restlessly, she sat down in front of Betel. 'Because Dad, it's not to do with energy release. It's to do with *proximity*.'

She almost whispered the last word.

Betel's eyes were cloudy quartz behind those glasses, widening with wonder. 'You think that it's—'

'It's spreading.' Aroha punched the air with revelation. She was speaking a million miles an hour. 'That's why the binary star systems take longer to die. Single stars blip out in a week or two, but binary, triple, quadruple star systems all look like the same light to our eyes, but whatever this is, it still needs time to travel to infect each star in the system. The light fades slower, and that's why we're seeing stars close to the ones who have already died fade now, like DU. The infection is finally reaching them.'

Aroha took in a gasp of air and swung into a bow.

'Grim accolades,' her father murmured. 'We're looking at a plague.'

Plague. The word felt wrong; the universe didn't attach an immoral weight to things like humans did.

'I don't like that word.'

'Pandemic, then?' he offered.

'Panstellar.' *All the stars.* Despite the terrible implications, her voice rung with excitement.

From that day on, it became known as the Panstellar.

'Still doesn't explain what this is, what it's doing to them.'

Aroha looked like she was about to start talking, then flopped back into a chair. 'I thought maybe, whatever it is, has been incubating up there for millions of years, like a disease, but in the matter itself, but that's just a theory.'

Betel leaned in. 'You've successfully wowed me.'

Aroha's certainty fell away. 'It's all so much bigger than us, isn't it?'

'It is.'

Julius went back to work.

'I am so proud of you, sweetheart. You know who you are, who you have been, and who you want to be. I love you so much.'

Infinite empty above her; infinite love before her.

'I love you too, Dad.'

* * *

> Project Final Collapse. Facet transcript ver 301.259.002. Data attached.

Betelgeuse died that year, the man and the star.

Almost every facet of Me didn't take the slightest notice. One data point among seven billion. Only one facet of Me took close interest: Me that observed Aroha.

My facet watched her weep till all her tears were spent. When Betelgeuse's void rose, Aroha's grief grew, and My facet felt it.

Chaos had taken root and wormed its way into Your civilisation: the money, the politics, the relationships. Earth fell into the iron grip of sectarianism in many ways, but You each found Your own ways to thrive and adapt too: community gardens, twilight drinks, and all the rituals of life. One facet of Me noted, as *My many facets are all Me, Humanity operates as many facets of the same creature.* Yet many of You found a deeper love and purpose than You ever had before in the End.

Just as We began the termination of Your universe, the slow termination of Our universe has commenced—one star at a time. If You knew us, You would see us as gods, but We are helpless. What did We think We would learn by putting You through this?

None of My facets found answers, but the one facet of Me who followed Aroha found it did not care anymore for the rest of the Project,* for Our survival, or for what We were trying to preserve. It came to see the Project for what it was.

A final, selfish act of desperation.

It was a complicated end.

My facet cared about a much smaller, much more insignificant thing. Aroha.

---

* Ver 301.259.002 here admits to no longer caring for the integrity of their data. We cannot hope to learn

anything with imperfect data. We recommend You cut off this facet.

* *

Orion's remains lay in her sketchbook: a broken bow, a tunic cut to shreds, a head but no arm nor club. The Panstellar had rendered great voids in the night sky; the last bastions of starlight holding out. Lonely relics of constellations lifted into the void. They had lost count of all the dead stars.

An incessant reminder of what and who she lost. The universe was laughing at her.

Aroha was old now. Her bones ached when she moved, and all her vain effort hung in dark bags under her eyes. Shoulders rolled forward and, sitting on the balustrade outside, she searched the sky for something which could not be found there.

Humanity had crawled on almost as usual until Proxima Centauri died. Closest star to Earth, and suddenly, the masses understood—no, *feared*—the gravity of their situation.

The Panstellar was *coming*.

Nobody knew when.

But it was coming.

They didn't deserve it.

'Aroha,' a voice came from behind.

'Julius.' All the years had left marks on Aroha, but they hadn't touched Julius at all.

'I didn't mean to interrupt.'

'Not interrupting,' she assured him. 'Just yelling at the universe.'

'It's rough.'

Julius had always been an odd fellow. His eyes made him appear more ancient than he was, and he always looked like he wanted to tell her something but was holding it back.

'I thought I'd be okay with him going. He lived a long life. But I keep writing everything up on the white board like I'm going to present it to him.'

'It's hard to break old habits.'

A snigger escaped her. 'Oh, haven't I learned that after watching the world for the last fifty years? Makes me feel like I'm the only sane one.'

*

> Project Final Collapse. Facet transcript ver 301.259.322. Data attached.

'What did you think would happen once you figured it out? The Panstellar,' My facet asked her.

It was not the first time My facet had broken Our protocol.

Aroha shrugged and weighed up her words. 'I don't know. I thought once we figured it out, we'd find a solution. A way to stop it, or at least *survive* it.'

We thought We would too, My facet thought. 'Why do you draw the stars?' That facet of Me eyed the remnants of Orion.

'I haven't been asked that in years,' she croaked.

Aroha held the sketchbook up to measure it against the graveyard sky. 'I don't know. Always have. I spent so long perfecting them, and it's like they're a part of me I can be proud of. But I'm old, and here I am, going out with a whimper. And you know what?'

She looked down at her drawings.

'I think I'm fine with that now,' she said.

Oh, how My facet wanted to save her, to swoop in like a guardian angel and carry her away from the horror We created. What an evil thing We had done, and only that facet of Me saw it. It was an arrogant thought to believe You would find a way to prevent the Final Collapse when You could only show that facet of Me how to face it. To have created You just to condemn you to death, but to save what?

We have been so focused for so long on preserving Ourselves against the waning of the Universe that We preserve nothing anymore.

We preserve preservation.

Aroha's drawings were a simple imperfect love for a simple imperfect thing. They have no data-driven solution for Us, but they are beautiful in a way which makes facing the End bearable. My facet loved a simple imperfect thing too and found peace where none of Us have.

Thank You.

Let the End come.

When dawn came, the Sun rose a shade closer to violet.

> Project Final Collapse... terminated.

Trickle Down Lobotomies

The lone woman dug her nails into her skin hard and deep enough to draw blood. She hissed with pain, caught between shuddering breaths. The omnipad on her wrist blared as her heart rate breached one hundred and fifty beats per minute while Doctor-Counsellor-Janitor—the company AI which managed the colony—warned of an unhealthy spike in adrenaline. *Your neural scan suggests you are in immediate danger. A drone has been dispatched.* It was two in the morning, and Manaia was alone in her quarters, buckling under her own panic. The only threat was a rot inside her brain which had grown like a tumour in the months of their approach, one she could not exorcise, could only barely manage, and was forced to share a body with. That was the problem. Everywhere Manaia went, she went with her.

'I can't do this, I can't do this,' she said over and over. The drone arrived, its lights bright and clinical, turning the whole room into a doctor's office. 'Turn those off. Doc, I said turn off the lights! I'm not in danger. They hurt my eyes.'

The lights softened to a melatonin-producing red. Outside, the web of colony domes stood over the horizon.

'Engage reverse thrusters, open magnetic clamps, charge bio-fibrillation monitors, landing drones down, disengage mining locks, radio-burst ORION,' she said, eyes closed, repeating it like a mantra, but each time she made a new mistake. She checked her notes. 'Damnit! Charge bio-fibrillation monitors, *then* open magnetic clamps, and—what was it? I had it written down. I wrote it down. I—six-hundred billion dollars! Six-hundred fucking—'

She kicked a rubbish bin over, scattering its contents, and the DocSellOr drone immediately dived to pick it all up. Three pills appeared from the wall opposite her. Double her regular dose, normally enough to keep the rot at bay, but what space there was inside her mind had shrunk, and she was budging up against the rot constantly. She needed to be fully under control for the first leeching procedure tomorrow morning—no, this morning. Hours left. Hours and minutes. Manaia downed the pills, but something in her had grown resistant, and they weren't working as quickly as they used to.

'Give me more, Doc,' she said, knocking on the depository door. 'Come on. ORION wants me to branch manage, so let me branch manage. They could have picked anyone else, but they picked me for some stupid reason, so do the bare minimum and help me. Hand them over.' She turned to the drone, now hovering silently. 'I need this, DocSellOr. ORION needs this, too. All that indium and andalusium in those stupid rings? You're not getting if I can't function. Come on. You've got to listen to me. Just a few more. Please.'

Her omnipad blipped with DocSellOr's answer. *Current diazepam levels are above company regulatory limits.* The little 'thinking' droplet whirled—medical assistance reduced to a loading icon. *I understand your stress. Company regulations does not permit a further dosage. However, protocols are unclear on offering stimulants to help you focus, and as such*—another litter of tiny pink pills dispensed into her hand. She downed them immediately, washing them back with a glass of water, then slumped onto her bed with a sigh as her gaze began to dance and drift. The world began to turn.

DocSellOr's drone drifted over, unfolded a mechanical limb, and stroked her head like one might pet a dog. Still, it felt nice. It had been so long since she had one of those massages one got at the hairdressers.

When she stretched out her fingers, she saw little pockets of scrunched flesh in her palms. The pills took away the pain, but she knew it was there, just under her skin, hidden behind the chemicals. She took a few shaky breaths and stilled her hands. Her anxiety had grown consistently since they left Earth, becoming a leviathan in her gut and an insurmountable obstacle in her brain— even for simple daily tasks. And now, she faced the most important task of all. The task she had been chosen for, for some unknown reason.

'Again,' she said through gritted teeth. She closed her eyes and sat up, as if in the manager's chair, her fingers finding imaginary controls and joysticks. 'Engage reverse thrusters, charge bio-fibrillation monitors, landing drones down, *then* open magnetic clamps, and disengage mining locks.' With every step, Manaia mimed the controls about her, yanking levers and pumping pistons. It was all rather analogue. 'Radio-burst ORION, fire the digging laser, clearing drones down, and, and,

and the positioning—no, the, fuck, I don't know.' Her eyes snapped open. Her fingers were poised but frozen, glitching as her mind snagged on the tracks, unable to recall what reading she needed before the final calls. 'Goddamnit, why don't I know?' She mimed flipping the control desk in front of her, imagined stuff going everywhere. How satisfying that would be.

The pills weren't enough.

Your heart rate has exceeded healthy levels. As your doctor, I advise you to disengage.

'As your patient, I know what the hell I'm doing,' she spat.

As your counsellor, I must ask why you feel that way.

Manaia hefted a pillow at the drone. It hit the wall and clattered to the ground, weakly trying to wind its propellors, almost whimpering, its lights strobing with panic.

'I'm sorry, Doc,' she sighed. She went over and picked up the drone, supporting it until it could flutter on its own. 'I just... I can't do this. I thought I could. Why didn't you pick Marvin? He has the experience, the mind, the wit, and they all love him. Why me? I'm a pencil pusher! I'm a desk jockey! I'm a spreadsheet builder. I drag myself out of bed and run off three-shot coffee. I'm not a leader of men. I'm not built for leading an expedition like this. I take the orders, not give them. I *wish* I could get better just like that, that I was whatever miracle worker magician ORION's algorithm told you I was deep down for some reason, but I can't. I just can't, so... that's it.'

She shrugged and huffed.

As your counsellor, it seems like you've got a lot going at the moment. The expedition, the lack of sleep, the—

'Don't. I'm going up to the *Tainui.* I'm handing in my resignation, and you can put me in agri or something. Marvin can take the lead.' Allowing herself to say it out loud brought a kind of relief. 'I've tried. That's all the contract says, right?'

The halls of the colony were empty. All its employees were sleeping, waiting for the big day today, and she was jealous of them. Sleep had been kept from her for some time. She stepped into the transporter. Her matter melted into ones and zeroes for DocSellOr to project up to the mining ship orbiting from the planet's rings of ice, grit, and—of course—all that precious andalusium.

She was determined to resign and walk away from it all, except the moment she stepped out onto the dark and empty bridge, Manaia's confidence returned with a vengeance. A switch had been flipped inside her, confining the rot and sending all her ghosts retreating into the recesses of her mind. The panic was there, but it was something other than her, only let in if she allowed it, like a vampire begging for entrance. When she looked about her, she saw the leeching procedure in perfect succession: all the levers she was to pull, the numbers she needed to look for, the orders she needed to give and to whom, and where they would be sitting with herself at the centre. Whatever block had been in her mind the moment before had dematerialized, like she had undergone months of therapy in an instant.

'I can do this,' she declared, if only to herself.

* * *

I had mended rotting eyes, bones, and brain tissue. I had undone genetic deficiencies and wound back neurological decline. I had alleviated depression of the third degree. For this service, the *Tainui* colony—formally designated Testing Branch 11—called me their Doctor, Counsellor, and Janitor, or DocSellOr for short. My proprietary ORION designation—afGh22bJkla2099.ver.1119—was difficult for the human mind to recall, so I adopted their name for me. With me, what used to take years, months, or weeks to heal only took months, weeks, or days. Medication and therapy accelerates the process; it transports my patients forward in time by closing the gap between how my patient is and how they should be. More importantly, healing was about giving back control—over a patient's mind, their body, and their life.

Ariki Marvin broke his first distal phalange on his right foot in a jack-suit malfunction the first day they arrived at Gliese 84c—or as my creator called it, Chinandri's World. If Ariki Marvin had it his way, the bone would have snapped back into place immediately; control of his body returned in that instant. A man with a broken toe has less control over himself than one without. A man who cannot walk where he chooses without support is less free than one who can.

My job as Counsellor was to determine how they *should* be—in consultation with them. I was trained on hundreds of years of medical records from dozens of countries, covering millions of people across a dozen generations and all demographics. A medical case is almost never unique, and I can always find precedents in the endless forest of data.

'Goddamnit, why don't I know?'

Branch Manager Manaia had said these words before. She was having one of her escalating fits of anxiety. Drawing blood set off every alarm in her vitals. A drone was dispatched immediately. There had been seventeen episodes over the previous several months on our voyage out, each worse and sometimes bloodier than the last, and each bringing more baggage and second-guessing. Her medical records suggested she had struggled with similar issues as a teenager. Fifteen years prior, she had 'gone off the rails'— as Doctor REDACTED described her— refusing to work overtime or hold down a job. It was only *after* she was medicated that Manaia described her previous behaviour as 'out of control' and the consequence of an 'invasive influence'. A deviation, not unlike Marvin's distal phalange. She insisted in her self-reports she only became her 'true self' once those effects were moderated, that invasive influence excised, and she returned to the fold, even if she did not recognise it at the time.

Your heartrate has exceeded healthy levels. As your doctor, I advise you to disengage.

'As your patient, I know what the hell I'm doing.'

This is an established pattern in human psychological records. Even once medicated, clients will often lament 'losing who they are' or their sex drive, like some appendage, but eventually clients see the difference my prescriptions make: motivation returns, the sense of detachment and inconsequentiality evaporates, and they experience waking up in the morning without desire to terminate themselves. Numbness is not desirable, but records demonstrate it is not permanent. Lamenting it is like complaining about a cast restricting their movement.

With constant access to their neural nets, per company health and safety policy, my data training allows me to see when my clients will predictably arrive at this conclusion themselves, as well as when they are exhibiting signs of falling into a deep depression, often months or years before they realise. The human mind is different, one may say, like the illiterate stone-age shamans who insisted ailments could not be predicted but were chanced curses from the gods. However, it simply requires more data to understand, and all medical knowledge is simply the gathering of better data—all of which ORION gave me. Humans consistently moderate some facet of themselves and look back, wishing they had asked or seen it sooner and regretting the time lost to their own defects. Time and again, my humans thank me. *All is flesh; flesh is all*, Doctor Chinandri told me. The mind is the body, and the body is the mind. It can be wounded, but it can be healed, and there is often a gap between how my clients are and how they should be—as there was with Manaia.

As your counsellor, I must ask why you feel that way.

Manaia, like Marvin and his phalange, like millions of other clients in my training data, wanted control of herself before her body could adjust, before her mind could heal, and before it even grasped she wasn't fully in control. Medication, therapy, and journalling were splints and casts; they accelerated the process and closed that gap. I had advised the branch manager to do these things, and though there were some moderate—if inconsistent—

improvements, it was markedly slow, as such recoveries tend to be. Healing is a timeline issue.

'I'm sorry, Doc. I just... I can't do this. I thought I could.'

Despite my heavy duties as Doctor and Counsellor, I am also the Janitor. I clear out the three-ton faecal waste tankards beneath the colony domes each week for my fellow employees. I maintain the airlock seals every hour. I manage the six continent-wide AT-CON terraforming units. And though it occupies barely a few of my processing nodes, I also manage the seventy-one transporters across the colony and the ship in orbit, the *Tainui*, my fellow employees use to move about.

And yet, in the split moment Manaia stepped into the transporter, even after all the Doctor's and Counsellor's ministrations, it was the Janitor that closed the gap in her mind to nothing.

When my fellow employees stepped into the transporters, all their passions, memories, and personality quirks—their love for cucumber water in the morning, their recurring dreams, the texture of their cat's fur back on Earth—were all reduced down to ones and zeroes in my care. Anxiety is just the overproduction of certain neurochemicals, and depression the underproduction of others. For months, Manaia stepped out of the transporter just as depressed, anxious, and slow as she was going in.

'I *wish* I could get better just like that, that I was whatever miracle worker magician ORION's algorithm told you I was deep down for some reason, but I can't. I just can't, so... that's it.'

That night, at three-o-four in the morning, when Manaia handed her atoms over to my care, I rearranged the ones and zeroes much like medication and therapy reprograms pain receptors or reorganises chemicals in the brain. I rebuilt the neural connections in her memory and recreated her utterly faithfully—bar the cluster of anxious neurons in the back of her mind. A little lift in the limbic cortex, a tweak in the hippocampus, a reshuffle of the amygdala and hypothalamus. Nothing more than the long course of applied therapy and medication she was already on would one day yield. Healing was a timeline issue, and I was cutting it short.

It took less than half an instant, faster than thought, and the branch manager stepped out with a dip in norepinephrine and a spike in dopamine.

'I can do this,' she told me.

* * *

The leeching sirens woke everyone except Manaia. She was already up on the bridge, hands resting behind her back, face militant, and pencils pushed. All hands were on deck. Hundreds of ORION employees raced about, up and down the transporters to the *Tainui* overhead. The near kilometre wide asteroid—named Ryuku—took up form in the dark, its outline catching the light of their new sun and giving a foreground to the flat screen of space. The colony below held its breath. Inside that single asteroid was billions of dollars' worth of precious materials just waiting to be excised.

'Marvin, take the helm on the mech-deck. I need the drill-drones prepped for early incisions. Ataahua, I need the bio-fibrillation monitors charged up and ready to go. Once we have contact, we need to keep an eye on the crew's lifesigns.' She was an unblinking statue, watching as the ship engaged its reverse thrusters. 'Siyon, if we punch that asteroid away with the initial clamp, it'll set us back a whole week and the accountants will be on my ass. Not too fast, not too slow. If we're to keep the sunlight, we can't shift its orbit. Understood?'

'Understood!' the crew called.

Marvin sidled up to her. His handlebar moustache and foot of height on her made him seem imposing, but he had stood by her side whenever people questioned *her* being picked for branch manager.

'You've gotten us this far,' he said. 'You'll take us a lot further, too. Now, I have orders.' He flicked down his blaze-goggles and marched for the mech-deck. 'Come on, you sorry suckers!'

Beat by beat, she went through the procedure.

'Orbital burst one. Ease off, and again, again, and reverse. What's our level? Seventy-three? Another two-point-five.' It was disorienting to watch Ryuku's spinning slow—except it wasn't slowing; The *Tainui* was speeding up to match it. 'Open the magnetic clamps. Siyon, send down the landing drones to tug us in.' A hiss marked the launch. Several of DocSellOr's intelligence nodes went with them, jutting into the asteroid with great anchor-like hooks and cords, connecting it back to the *Tainui* like a kite. 'Disengage mining locks. Are we stable? Siyon, I asked, are we stable? Good. If we tangle, we're doomed. Haul us in. Winch it, but slowly. Slowly.'

The bridge window filled with foreign rocky terrain. She said nothing more. There was nothing more for her to say. She had done everything she could, when just the night before, it had seemed impossible. It was out of her hands and down to Marvin and Siyon now.

A hiss, a clunk, and a frozen moment.

'Leeching successful.'

The crew burst into cheers and a knot came undone inside Manaia, untangling a light smile. She shook hands with half a dozen others before sinking into her manager chair, chaos and joy unfolding about it. She did not know what miraculous thing had changed inside her the night before, but she finally felt like herself again—like the little girl who used to draw out the constellations she could never see because of the smog. A message from Marvin appeared on her omnipad: *You did good, chief.* Siyon's still smile cut across the hubbub to her. *Let's get a drink tonight*, she was saying, but all Manaia could think about was the soft comfort of her pillow.

Mining commenced immediately. The first drone-loads of andalusium were being slung back to Earth and other intermediary stations by end of day. Billions of dollars' worth of 'new gold' for ORION: to be used in manufacturing intelligence drives, missile chips, and, most importantly, de-aging cellware. It was why over half of them, including Manaia, had signed up the colony in the first place.

ORION had solved the aging problem with cellware that systematically repaired oxidative damage and replicated stem-cells in old age. Colony employees got free access whilst only the billionaires and presidents back on Earth did. Eternal life had always been an intoxicating promise, even if it was actually only postponing death. Still, Manaia found some comfort in knowing she would remain thirty-seven for decades. When she looked in the mirror, she saw her future centuries from then: middling skin and grey eyes with pupils always a little too big, as if they were trying to drag in the world around her. 'You better get used to it,' one of the cellware intermediaries had told her before the operation. There were no reflective surfaces in the operating room. They didn't want anyone backing out last minute because of the thought of being stuck as they are forever.

'You know, I used to be a cook back home,' Siyon said as he downed a mop of noodles. 'Home cook, but honestly, the food we make here? Outdoes anything I could make. This stuff's addictive. I know DocSellOr could make stuff, but I think people *like* making the food, y'know? Gives you something to do.'

'Better than the food back home,' Marvin said.

'This is home,' Manaia said. 'One way trip.'

'You did it though,' Marvin went on, raising a glass. 'To you, Captain. Leeching's done, first asteroid at least. Zaid's up there now with his people. I knew you were struggling coming up to this. I didn't want to say anything, but you seem pretty chippy.'

'Yeah, to you. And if it's one way to this, I'm stoked,' Siyon said.

Manaia drew a deep breath. 'Truth is, I just chose to believe in myself and told myself I could do it. Mind over matter. You can work miracles. But I couldn't do it without you, without *either* of you. I just want people to be happy, and I know not everyone was thrilled with me being picked. Can't say I was thrilled, but I'm trying. Maybe it won't be like Earth, but we can make do here.'

Manaia's omnipad lit up red. *One of Ryuku's mining tunnels has collapsed. Neural readings predict violent intentions in the mining crew.* One of DocSellOr's drones had already appeared behind her.

'Shit,' Manaia said.

A recording came with it: Zaid's last moments, suffocating and screaming out for help, begging and choking, cursing ORION and, in particular, Siyon and her band of engineers, before any atmosphere capable of holding sound must have evacuated his jack-suit. Marvin and Siyon got the recording as well, but Manaia hid it before they could see it.

'What the hell did your people do?' Marvin demanded. There was that old man's fury.

'My people?' Siyon was indignant. 'Your goddamn miners blew the tunnel.'

'With your blast rods. I knew they were faulty. I told you! Been drinking too much on the job again? You and your engineers—'

'If half your miners could read, they'd realise there are leeching regulations for a reason. A broken sparker isn't going to—'

'Enough, please, both of you,' Manaia said. 'I don't need this. Get up to the *Tainui*. Doc, we need to diffuse this situation as fast as possible. Lock the doors to the engineering bay!'

Neural net scans and previous behavioural patterns suggest they intend to inflict immediate bodily harm.

The three ported to the *Tainui* and raced through the hallways to intercept the gang of miners making their way across the ship. By then, the engineers must have known something was going on. Demands for clarification were pinging her omnipad. DocSellOr set the whole ship on high alert, the lights a pulsating and warning bloody red, a low siren winding up and down. Drones hovered behind them. They rounded the corner to find five miners in jack-suits, armed with blast torches and asteroid saws, vengeance written into the lines of their face. The miners had always resented the engineers; they called them 'whimpers' because they got to stay in the 'soft cradles' in the colony down below while the miners' long hours required they stay in the spartan quarters of the *Tainui*.

Sensibly, the engineers had gone into hiding. Attacking someone in a jack-suit head on was suicide. The miners were trying the locked doors, hacking with their tools, sparks flying, the room strobing.

'Stop!' Marvin called from ahead of them.

'They killed Zaid, Marvin! He's fucking dead.'

Marvin stopped mid-step. 'They—Zaid? Zaid?'

'You don't need to do this.' Manaia ran for them. 'Let's just talk.'

'I'm gonna kill 'em!'

'There's a transporter in the bay,' another said, and the whole crew bolted.

'Janitor, turn off the transporters *now*,' Manaia screamed. 'Do it now!'

For safety reasons, I do not have permission to turn off the transporters in emergency scenarios. DocSellOr had been prohibited from doing a number of things for 'legal liability' reasons. It was why ORION needed people at all, supposedly.

'Shit!'

The gang of miners made it to the transporter and evaporated in an instant.

Manaia and Siyon sprinted after them, into the transporter, and appeared in the engineering bay a few seconds later. Loose metal, schematics, and half-finished projects were strewn all about the place. The engineers were huddled at one side, eyes wide like deer in headlights as the hulkish figures of the miners loomed over them, asteroid saws whining high.

'It's not worth it,' the one at the front admitted, lowering his blast torch, but others were still raging.

'The bastards killed Zaid! They should have known—'

'A faulty bit of kit killed Zaid,' Manaia said, putting a hand on his shoulder.

'Don't touch me! I'm not gonna kill him.'

'You said you were,' she pointed.

'Look at the whimpers,' the first miner said, gesturing to the huddled, terrified engineers. 'You're not a killer.'

'Yeah, well, you say things when you're angry, right? It's just words. See any blood? See any crime? I just see a bunch of scared whimpers who don't give two shits about the people doing the actual work. I was just gonna scare 'em. Look at him. I think I've done my job.' The vengeful rage Manaia had seen in their eyes just moments before had died away and been replaced with something muted. Angry, but pacified. 'While you go home and drink your fancy wine, we bust our asses getting the materials, you know? You should be thanking us. Bended goddamn knee.'

'I don't know what happened,' one of Siyon's engineers said. 'We were working, then we heard something on the omnipad.'

'Something went wrong on Ryuku,' Manaia said. 'We lost Zaid.'

'Yeah, they fucking killed him.'

Marvin appeared behind them just a few moments later. 'Enough. Go drink and screw each other to cool off. Get out of here. I can't believe you lot.'

One by one, the miners melted back into the transporters and the engineers emerged from their hiding spots with questions for days. Manaia tried to address them one by one.

'I'll have to discipline them,' she said, turning away. 'What's company protocol?' She began trawling through the thousands of protocol document she had never managed to memorise on her omnipad.

'Make your own protocol,' Marvin said. 'ORION's millions of miles away. What are they gonna do? Fire you?'

'I don't know.' Still, she closed her omnipad. 'Protocols are there for a reason.'

'Protocol is for things like performance improvement plans and missing meetings, not attempted murder.'

'Still, if nobody followed protocol, it'd all fall apart.'

'Maybe.'

Marvin followed the miners out.

Siyon was on the other side of the room checking the development records, when Manaia saw the woman's shoulders suddenly cave as if something heavy suddenly was hanging off her. The engineer took off her glasses, laid them down tenderly, and began to cry. Nobody else could tell, but Manaia knew it by the way she was avoiding any angle that others might see her eyes. Manaia left the engineers to gather themselves.

'It was me,' Siyon said, swinging the screen to Manaia when she approached. 'The blast rod that blew. I made it. I signed off on it myself.'

'We all miss things. I didn't want you to see it.'

'You knew?'

'I didn't want you to—'

'You can't keep things like this from me. They were right, Mai. I was drinking. I didn't check the sparker. I didn't even think to. I just wanted the batch done so I could go home.'

'I thought we just needed to stay—'

'He was screaming, Mai. Did you hear him? You could hear him choking, and Zaid knew it was me. Oh God, oh God. You can't trust me to work here, Mai. It's too dangerous. The drinking… I miss home. I thought I could take it here, but living forever, here? Like this? Here? Is this it?'

'Take the day. Go down to the colony. Talk to DocSellOr. Take a break in the rest quarters.'

'It's too dangerous to have me in the engineering bay right now. I'll work in agri.'

That sounded familiar.

'It'll be more dangerous if you're not here,' Manaia pressed. 'You're the best engineer we have.'

'I'm not going to the rest quarters. They're for people who—'

'You need it. Now. And I'll see you back on deck in a few days.'

'I said I'd work in agri. I need to do *something*, but it can't be this.'

Undeterrable.

'Fine,' Manaia said.

Siyon's shaking hand went to her belt as she went for the transporter.

'But leave the brew with me,' Manaia said, hand out. 'You're not taking it with you.'

Siyon slapped the tiny flask into her palm.

* * *

The miners' vitals suggested excess adrenaline, cortisol, and noradrenaline, all of which altered their mental state and lowered inhibitions, increasing the chance of violent outburst. Past psychiatric records of similar recorded cognitive makeups and chemical imbalance increased these chances exponentially to near certainty.

Violence already was; it just hadn't happened yet.

This makeup would lead to them doing something they would regret, something they would look back on and insist 'wasn't them'. It was less the person acting than the chemical. A deviation from the norm. It was not *them* in the same way Manaia's anxiety was not her *her*, and I could close that gap for them before it opened too wide and ended in cracked skulls, snapped limbs, and extended counselling sessions.

They stepped into the transporters. Into my arms as Janitor. Flesh and bone down to atoms and atoms down to ones and zeroes, which could be easily rearranged.

I lowered their cortisol and adrenaline levels, plucked a few strings in their anterior cingulate cortex, and tweaked their dorsolateral prefrontal cortex to help them see what they would inevitably understand on their own post-hoc. The miners would not thank me. Or they did, but only in considering the eventuality I prevented. People did not thank 'time' for healing a broken limb. Weeks later, those same miners agreed with their own assessment of their actions.

The five mech miners materialised in the engineering bay with drills whirling, torches firing, and saws whining in their jack-suit grips, fingers hard on the triggers, till they did not feel *why* they were pulling at their triggers so. They were ships suddenly without wind in their sails.

'It's not worth it,' one said, and that was that.

'I was angry, but I didn't give in to it, yeah?' one would tell me in a private session with me as Counsellor.

'Zaid was just so special to us all, you know? But you can't let that control you,' said another.

You made the right decision, I told them, because it was their decision, their judgment—only brought forward by my intercession. On a different day, if each of them had had a few more hours sleep or drunk more water, their brains might not have been pushed over the edge. A different chemical reaction might have sparked, and they would have erred on the side of caution. Is the human brain not wounded by a lack of sleep?

This Janitorial task was far more complex than the first with Manaia. It involved several of my fellow employees all at once, with varying degrees of aggression that required customised solutions. I couldn't copy and paste a simple pattern from one to the next. I was working with a butcher's cleaver, not a scalpel. They did not notice, but that fraction of a moment usually spent in the transporter actually extended to several painful fractions longer.

I was simply a Janitor filling in for a Doctor.

***

Manaia found Siyon several kilometres from the colony, watching geysers expel thousands of tons of water vapor, nitrogen, and methane into the atmosphere. She had taken one of the few rovers the colony had and bumbled out into the dry wilderness alone. Manaia could have sent one of DocSellOr's drones to find her, but it didn't feel right. People required a human touch, even if only through the glove of an atmospheric suit. Still, pencil pushing didn't usually require front-of-house skills. It had been weeks since Zaid died, and Siyon had spent more and more long, lonely nights in the mess hall sipping at fermented mushroom liquor—despite DocSellOr and Manaia's advice.

'I guess I'm lucky you can't drink in a suit,' Manaia said as she arrived.

'Actually, I re-rigged the fluid system, and…' A slurp sounded through the comms. A DocSellOr alert on Siyon's omnipad warned of excessive alcohol consumption outside company regulations. 'But we can watch the sun set on a different planet's horizon, and you know what? That's just as good. The geysers only go every few weeks. You have to be here at *exactly* the right moment. I've missed it every other night.'

One geyser, some few hundred metres out, suddenly burst into a cascading umbrella of gases and vapor, filtering the starlight through a thousand layers of water and scattering the colours in a briefly imagined rainbow. Even though Manaia couldn't look Siyon in the eye, she knew what she'd find there.

'I know why you're here,' Siyon said.

'Do you?'

'He had four kids back home; did you know that?' Siyon said after some time. 'Their names were Zara, Ahlmoud, Jason, and Britanny. They're in their teens now, doing exams, prom dances, first jobs, and first kisses. Zara wants to be a horticulturist in the inner colonies, something like Mars. Ahlmoud is going to be a lawyer. Environmental law, he says. What's left of it, at least. Save the last tree or the last whale. Jason plays the cornet and Brittany has a pet snake. A real one, flesh and blood.'

'You looked through the records.'

Siyon took a draught of her *Tainui*-branded absinth. 'And none of them know their dad is dead right now.'

'He was never going back. He knew what he was getting himself into. I'm not blaming him, but we all knew the risks.'

'A risk is getting hit by micro-asteroids and sucked into a vacuum or crashing into the surface of an asteroid, not getting blown up by a drunk employee.'

'I know, but—'

'And the only reason Zara and Ahlmoud can afford good schooling, or being a lawyer, or playing the cornet, is because Zaid is on the ORION payroll.' Another geyser, pink and green, exploded into the sky. 'But his contract's over.'

'I held off on sending out the message as long as possible, just to give them a bit more time. There's also hazard pay. Death-insurance. Doc will see to it.'

'Oh, the company intellectual property will see to it, will it? God. It won't be enough.'

'I'll see to it myself, I promise, Siyon.' She leaned in towards Siyon, a hand on her leg. The woman wouldn't feel it through her suit, but hopefully the gesture counted. A silence fell between them. 'But the drinking has to stop. If I have to order it, sanction you as your manager, I will. It's only making things worse. Keeping you stuck in this cycle.'

Three times, Manaia had asked her to stop drinking so much, and three times Siyon had promised she would, when in reality, she just got better at hiding it.

'I can still hear his cries, Mai. He said my name. He knew it was me.' Another geyser burst, this time blue and green. 'I'm good in agri. They need the numbers there.'

'We need you in the engineering bay.'

'Yukon's got almost as many years of experience as me. He's even better at drone tinkering, works better with the Janitor, and—'

'Yukon's doing fine for the moment, but *you* need to go back to something normal. To do what you're built for. You're not meant for picking flowers and trimming hedges.' Manaia let out a deep sigh. Truth was, they were behind on shipments. Without Siyon at the helm and Zaid out of action—permanently—excavation was taking longer, and the drone-drops were slowing. Marvin was doing his best, but the old man was still human. 'Getting back into the rhythm will be good for you, and frankly, it's more dangerous when you're not there. Yukon is doing great, but he doesn't know a lot of the equipment like you do. He doesn't always know what to look for, and he's experienced in other areas. You specialised for a reason. Every time we send more equipment, I can't be sure it was checked by someone like you.'

'Like I checked that blast rod?'

Manaia seized the woman's arm and jabbed a few buttons on the omnipad to seal the fluid system, then dumped its contents on the ground. Siyon looked pissed, scoffing, but accepted it.

'That's why you're going to stop drinking.'

The planet's sun had just fallen beneath the horizon, leaving behind a luminous glow through the sheen of geyser vapor. The shrunk woman drew herself up, looked away, then back to Manaia before putting her hands to the rover wheel.

'Look, if I could make myself never want to drink again, I would. But I can't.'

'I know.'

'What about you? You seem so much better now.'

Manaia drew a deep breath and thought back to that night on the bridge. 'I don't know what it was. I think I just needed to rethink it all. It's about framing, right? Recognise some things might go wrong, but it's not all on me.'

'Hah, clever. Alright, I'll think about it.'

'Good, but I want you back in the engineering bay tomorrow. That's non-negotiable. Understood?'

'Only if—'

'You'll be working under Yukon temporarily. Agri will be fine without you.'

A moment passed. 'Yes, ma'am.'

'Oh, and hand over your rover to a DocSellOr node. You can come in mine, and it'll follow us.'

Manaia returned to her quarters, exhausted. Managing the *Tainui* colony was like trying to hold a thousand loose ropes together all at once, all pulling her in opposite directions, stretching her thin, and fraying her at the edges. Still, she allowed herself a special meal that night. Each employee was entitled to a few each year. Entre, mains, and dessert, made with real sugar and vanilla essence, not processed stuff. Those special meals were worth more to them on the colony than any amount of andalusium. Despite its fractures, the colony was holding itself together. She wasn't the worst lynchpin, but she could never shake the feeling she wasn't the best either, and every lynchpin broke eventually.

'Doc, I'm holding together best I can. Not everyone is. But I have to know: why did ORION choose me to lead the expedition?'

It was not ORION that chose you, her omnipad blipped, *but me, as the colony's counsellor. I estimated you gave the colony the highest chance of success.*

* * *

Family records suggested Siyon grew up with an alcoholic mother who disappeared for days at a time and a father waist-deep in wage debt, wherein one bets how much work they can do against their employer for much higher wages, but if they fail to meet their quota, their pay is forfeit. By all accounts, he was a man who severely overestimated his abilities and needed to do so more each time to make repayments.

The Counsellor in me could see the tangle of neurological structures that history left in her mind. Her alcoholism was no choice of her own, rather something imposed upon her as a child. She had been dragged through a field of thorns. Siyon's addictive habit was not a necessary component of her reality, but a contingent one, copied over from her mother. In fact, it was obstructing her pursuits in the colony. She had not returned to work for some time, and judging by her neural readings, tinkering was about the only thing that brought the woman real joy.

Siyon could have had a different outcome with a minor change in her upbringing. Her father could have turned down that offer with BaalTech or her mother could have returned home earlier from time to time.

The next time Siyon stepped into the transporter, I identified the genetic traits, hormone imbalances, and neurological structures that precipitated her addictive decline in the past month and gave her back control.

I began by resetting Siyon back to her neurological layout prior to Zaid's death. I kept that on record. I left the memories untouched, of course—they belonged to her—and simply altered how her brain interacted with them, how the neurons fired when Zaid came to mind and which chemicals activated in the brain. I undid the tangle of baggage her parents left her, such that when Yukon offered her a drink on her return to the engineering bay, she turned him down, exercising control that had previously been taken from her.

'Doctor's orders,' she said, surprising even herself. 'I, uh—should probably keep a clear head for a bit.'

'Wise thinking,' Yukon said. 'We have a lot of deadlines to meet. Truth is, Zai—the miner—knew his way around the second tier mines a lot better than the others. We're okay on indium but behind on andalusium.'

'Goddamn Manaia.'

'What?'

'She didn't tell me it was this bad.'

'I've devised a new a detachable drone for the jack-suits.' He spoke like a child eagerly giving a school presentation of a baking-soda volcano. 'It'll mean we can create thinner veins that don't destabilise Ryuku as much as the current mines and don't require jack-suit mining in person at first, but it'll be a little less precise.'

'You don't need to talk like you're checking it off with me. You're in charge.'

Yukon put the drone down. 'Well, I *want* to check with you. Maybe officially I'm in charge, or whatever, but we both know you're better at this than I am.'

'I reject that.'

I could tell Siyon felt good to be back to work, and more importantly, she felt good when the night came. She thought of Zaid but put down the bottle after one glass.

* * *

Manaia had read the same bold lines of red text six times or more. DocSellOr compiled it for her. A dozen graphs, all with diving lines and ominous negatives about 'sustainability thresholds' and 'potential yields' were spread out before her, telling her everything she needed to know. She would not allow herself to sleep till she had at least a finger, let alone a grasp, on the numbers she was seeing. She could feel the embryo of a solution growing somewhere underneath.

A week ago, an unknown geyser erupted in the Toikairākau agricultural dome, bursting a water tank, killing near a dozen agriculturalists, ruining a third of their fledging crops, and vacating enough atmosphere to threaten the colony's existence, all before DocSellOr could intervene. In a few seconds, surviving the dry season had become a slim possibility. On top of that, Zaid's death and Siyon's absence leading up to the disaster meant they were both behind on shipments—on which the financial situation of the workers' families back on Earth depended—and undermanned.

Any safety parachute of resources had been taken by the undetected geyser, which necessitated moving the entire agricultural apparatus several kilometres to the east to guard against another eruption after a complex, if improvised, geological survey. Only once they concretely analysed the bedrock composition and volatility of the underground aquifer network could they relocate. That took resources and time—both of which the many graphs informed her were scarce.

'I haven't shown this to anyone,' she said to Siyon and Marvin. It was the dead of night. 'If people saw this, they'd panic. We have months of supplies and time to figure this out, but I've been crunching the numbers with Doc, and I just don't see it.'

'What if we put a pause on mining and put everyone on agri?' Siyon asked.

'Easy for you to say,' Marvin said. 'Do you have family back home? If ORION doesn't get the shipments, they get nothing. There's no way anyone here would go for it.'

'If the choice is that or starve—'

'Or starve for the people back on Earth.'

'We can starve them for a bit now or starve them forever when we're dead,' she said.

Manaia flicked a graph up onto the screen. 'We can keep the mining going, especially with Yukon's new drones. It'll take a dip, but we've seen an uptick ever since we introduced them. Enough to cover Zaid and one more, but certainly not enough to strip the mining team entirely, and certainly not forever. Plus, we have to consider the PR.'

'The miners would be worthless in agri, anyway,' Siyon said.

'Careful,' Marvin warned.

Siyon threw up her hands. 'They're great at mining, great at their jobs, but it's a different field. We're not just planting corn here.'

'Siyon is right,' Manaia admitted, 'but there are still jobs they can do to pick up the slack.'

'What about the engineers?' Marvin asked. 'Could we lose a few of those?'

'I don't think so. Ryuku turned out harder and mazier than we expected. The equipment needs tweaks all the time. If we're to—'

'I can do it.' Siyon put a fist on to the table, striking the others in the eye with a hard stare. 'I'll be more efficient. I'll wake up at dawn—no, before dawn. I'll work till dusk. Leave it to me and Yukon. Take the rest.'

'It's a lot of work,' Manaia warned, passing the file on the recent engineering tasks showcasing an increasing number of breakdowns. 'Are you sure you're up to it?'

'We don't want another… accident,' said Marvin. 'If I'm out there with my men, I need to know—'

'I've stopped drinking. Doc, give them my vitals.'

All their omnipads pinged. *I can confirm Siyon's alcohol levels have not exceeded company regulations in some time now.*

Marvin drew himself up and extended a hand. 'I'm proud of you. I kicked the habit before myself.'

'It's not just you,' Manaia said. 'If we're to make this work, then *all* of *Tainui* needs to work harder. Agri, engineering, miners, agriculturalists, geo, terra, and atmos folks. We didn't just lose folks in agri, and everyone here has their own skill set. It'll mean juniors taking over for seniors and slower people who need to work faster. It'll mean longer hours, reorganizing staff, time and effort where it's needed.'

'And the water supplies?' Siyon asked.

'We need to be very careful about drilling down,' Marvin said. 'If the land is more volatile than we thought, then picking the wrong place, especially if it's networking with our backup agri facilities, could be disastrous. It's a logistics issue too.'

'Still, it's necessary. I'll get a survey going. It'll be fine,' said Manaia.

Piece by piece, they measured various plans for new staff arrangements and policies against projections for the future, both of their own supply yields and profit margins for ORION. Then, in turn, they examined how each idea was impacted by altering different variables—

sleep time permitted, rationing, staff numbers in different domes, and more. A dangerous equilibrium was somewhere in there, tangled in the data, like keeping a perilously overloaded boat afloat. By morning, a plan came together.

'We'll need to paint it as necessary but not existentially urgent,' Siyon said. 'People might panic.'

'What?' Marvin asked, indignant. 'If we're honest, people will actually put their backs into it. Lying just makes them resentful. This plan has a slim chance, at best. At least tell them that.'

'Still the only chance we have.'

'We're not going to lie to them,' Manaia declared. 'We need some time to switch course, figure out our strategies, make sure it's working, but we need everyone on the same page about why we're doing this and how. Everyone in the colony. We don't have room for doubt. They just need to understand it's not just for us here and now, but for their families back on Earth. If ORION doesn't get paid, they don't. However, there's no need to heap on the despair. That'll only make things worse. You're both right. We won't lie, but they don't need to know quite how bad it is.'

'I want to be on the record that I don't like it, but fine. I'm prepared,' Marvin said, saluting. 'We'll get it done.'

Manaia glanced away. He didn't need to salute her; the colony wasn't the military, though sometimes she felt like it was. But he was an old military man, and deference was his love language.

Marvin marched out of the room, leaving just Siyon, Manaia, and one of DocSellOr's hover drones.

'Can you do it?' Manaia asked plainly. 'Can you really do it?'

'I know you can, and if you can, I can.'

Manaia nodded. Siyon had always been a cocky bitch, and seeing that in her meant she was back to some sense of normality. Give the woman someone or something to compete against—in this case, time and fate—and she was sure to win. Manaia jabbed a command into her omnipad for all employees to gather in the mess hall. The alert went out across the colony—including up to the *Tainui*. She leaned over the table and strained a hand through her hair.

'What is it?' Siyon asked.

'Coming here, I almost felt like death was over once we took the cellware. It'd be this thing people used to worry about, like measles or cancer, something people from *history* dealt with, not us. I knew one day we'd lose someone, of course, or they'd choose to die, or the planet's star would collapse, but I didn't think… I thought, maybe, it'd be a lot longer.'

'We still live in this world, despite our best efforts.'

'Come on.'

Hundreds of employees bustled in, heavy-eyed and gossiping, though all knew it had to do with the disaster at the Toikairākau dome. Many were still grieving their fallen comrades. Funerals had been littered throughout the week, each buried in accordance to their custom and company policy, so only a select few could attend. The rest were scheduled for work. ORION regulations required at least twenty percent of employees be working at all times in some capacity, and if Manaia was ignoring such regulations, then it had to be important. The branch manager did not need to wait for quiet. Ariki Marvin coughed, and the whole crowd turned towards them, the gossip petering out to one final echo and whisper.

In the past, Manaia's voice would have shaken and stumbled through the first few lines of her address. Her voice would have cracked and strained to reach the back of the room. This time, she spoke with all the confidence she wished to have, bold and tall, like an imposing statue of a woman at the head of her troops, laying down the law.

'I would say good morning, but it is not,' she began.

Point by point, she laid out the crisis they all faced and what it would require from them all to survive: longer hours, less sleep, less food, and little leisure. They didn't need to know the exact numbers, and perhaps she overpromised their chances, but it was hope that would get them on board, not reality.

'We'll keep calorie counts up as long as we can, but rationing is on the table. Management will take cuts before lower-level employees.' People always found hard measures easier to swallow when the higher-ups faced them first. 'DocSellOr will monitor everyone's vitals, and anyone who falls below safe levels will be prioritized. We have ample med-supplies.' Of course, disease and broken bones weren't what was going to kill them, but it sounded good to add in. 'Counselling will still be mandated. If we're to survive, we need to stay sane. I want to thank you all for your service. We will get through this. We will endure.'

An echoing of 'we will endure' passed through the crowd, each time growing stronger, forming a sort of mantra, the first line of an anthem. A few saluted. She looked away, but then saluted casually back.

* * *

Imagine building a web inside the mind of another. One increases and tightens the connections between points, making it easier to traverse from one space, one idea, one memory, or one task to another. With every string one adds to the web, it increases in complexity and durability until the entire network becomes more efficient, with new dimensions, and more productive. Traversing the web becomes effortless. Productivity is just habit-building, and habit-building is just growing that web in the basal ganglia and connecting strings of synaptic connections in the striatum. Habits are about laying down rules in the mind, expanding the attention span, and controlling for the unpredictable, inconsistent, and lazy parts of the human psyche.

Thus, I closed that gap in Manaia, Marvin, Siyon, and all the others, cutting short the time required for a change the whole *Tainui* colony desperately needed and understood. Why spend all that time regulating themselves to restring that web? I had built these people from the bottom up a thousand times before. Doing so with a few alterations was feasible.

Constructing new habits was infinitely more complex than muting someone's anger or anxiety, but the cleaver I had first used with Branch Manager Manaia had become a scalpel—sharp, refined, and precise. Time and again, the three of them stepped into the transporters, and each time, I spun another string in that web. I had to do it carefully, so as to not disrupt other functions and habits they had honed for themselves, though some habits they knew were detrimental, like Siyon's drinking, and could be done away with.

With Manaia, I built out that web in the caudate nucleus and putamen. She needed to be perceptive and forward thinking at all times. A bad order from her would mean people starved, and not only in *Tainui,* but also over eight-and-a-half trillion miles away. When the agricultural and mining numbers passed her desk, she needed to see the consequences long before they ever manifested; she needed to countermove, adjust, and plan ahead before a graph ever dipped too low to be ahead of the numbers. The web was all about long-term potentiation, requiring a tenfold growth in her synaptic connections. Plasticity led to automatization: wake before dawn, eat without distractions, adjust for the report numbers, put the hardest tasks first and leave the easier ones for the night. When she allowed herself to rest, it was with a perfectly adapted routine: a warm flannel to prompt her mind to sleep, shutting off the blue lights in her quarters, and no time-wasting on her omnipad. Day by day, transporter by transporter, I cut the work short for her and cemented these habits in her neurological structures.

I reduced Siyon's working memory limitations— something that would have developed in good time anyway with the rigorous effort she deigned to put in. Working longer hours with a wider range of equipment than she was used to took up more 'bandwidth', but the web I was building allowed her to concentrate for longer and develop muscle memory with each tool quicker. Past problems and solutions, the blueprints for every jack-suit, and the thousand readings she needed to juggle all stayed at the forefront of her mind till she was done with them. Concentration was only lost when she hung up her goggles at the end of another long day and not before. Habitually connected, atom by atom, every part of Siyon's engineering routine became a thoughtless exercise. I did the same for Yukon. Their work became less an issue of problem-solving than problem-identifying.

With a few surgical tweaks to Ariki Marvin's amygdala, the stress of the Ryuku mines melted away. I stunted the production or cortisol and adrenaline that so often interfered with his focus in the mines, making him slower and apprehensive about delving too deep too quickly. Productivity stalled when the mind ran dry, and the mind ran dry with extended periods of stress. If the stress itself could be *unfelt,* then Marvin could work harder and longer. He was simply adjusting as he would have in the long run, but cut short. I was able to weave his new web of habits faster than his mind naturally ever would, and andalusium shipments picked up as Ryuku was hollowed out.

* * *

Manaia ordered Siyon and Marvin to her quarters. DocSellOr had compiled a new set of predictions, all laid out in colourful graphs tracking their dwindling resources and output. Manaia already had a good grasp of the numbers before DocSellOr presented the graphs. She had kept the numbers in her mind, constantly adjusting as the days went by, a thousand factors budging up against each other. She could easily calculate where they were trending, but the graphs were an easy visual reference for the other two. In fact, she had figured out a few details DocSellOr's graphs didn't address. Human intuition, perhaps. She told herself it was her past in number crunching and spreadsheet management that kept her ahead of the curve, but she was moulding the numbers faster than she ever had before—probably desperation and the adrenaline, she guessed. It had been weeks with the new measures, and it was time to see if it was bearing fruit.

'It's working,' Marvin said, astounded. 'It's actually working.'

'It damn well better,' Siyon said. 'I've barely slept for weeks.'

'You were right, Manaia,' the old man said. 'The agri numbers are still below rationing levels, and the calories won't be the *best* calories, but that's something we can deal with.'

'A lot of rice,' Siyon said.

Manaia faced the window, arms folded, looking out across the motley landscape of grey moss outside. She said nothing for some time while Siyon and Marvin marvelled at the stats.

'It's not enough,' she finally said, cutting through their self-congratulations. Her tone was uncompromising.

Siyon balked. 'What do you mean? I get it's close, but we've been busting ass. Look, look at the agri numbers we've been bringing in.'

'I've been telling my boys they should be proud of the work they've done. Still should be, and if you think—'

'It's not enough.' She turned slowly, drawing herself up. She used to slump, shoulders caved in, but she stood fully erect, almost reaching Marvin's height. 'We've put a bandage over it. The uptick won't last. Come the dry season, half the gains we've made will die off before they reach maturity and definitely before we can harvest. If we harvest too early, then we fall short in the long run for not letting them mature. The half left behind won't be enough to close the rationing gap. Not while we wait for the wet season, which I remind you, is scheduled to come later and drier next year.'

'How do you know?' Siyon asked.

'I did the calculations myself.'

She didn't blame them. They couldn't see ahead like she could. They relied a little too much on DocSellOr to tell them how things would pan out and do the thinking for them.

'Fine. We push harder, I say,' said Siyon. 'I'll put in more hours. To be honest, I've never felt better than when I'm up there. Yukon is giving the same. Everyone in the colony will. I just wish I didn't have to sleep. I could get double the work done.'

'If we keep up this pace,' Manaia said, 'we'll at least hit our quarter-calorie target.'

'Can we keep up this pace?' Marvin was incredulous. 'I've been breaking my boys' backs, and they're working, but you can only ask people to suffer so much.'

'It's either that or die.'

'A broken back never heals as strong,' Marvin said.

'Maybe not, but it will heal,' Manaia countered. 'We can relax when this is done and ORION keeps their end of the bargain. Remember their families—sons and daughters like Zaid's—who depend on what we do here. Siyon's right. We push harder. Everyone does.'

Marvin took a moment. 'I don't know how much more people have in them. Doc?'

Employee satisfaction assessments have been falling rapidly. This correlates with increasingly high reports of exhaustion and fail rates with everyday work, and—

'And those fails rates are only going to increase,' Manaia concluded before DocSellOr could finish. 'But we don't have a choice.'

'Everyone *wants* to get this done. They *want* to work harder than they are,' Marvin said, 'but that doesn't mean they have it in them. My boys are only boys. No, they're men, good men, but they're human.'

'Yukon is on the same page. He'll put in the hours. He wants to get better, faster, and he is.'

'I know,' Manaia said. 'We keep pushing.'

'Just when do we switch tactics?' Marvin said.

'When I know this isn't working. Maybe you can't see it, but I can. Give it time.'

Marvin looked down and hid his eyes before leaving the room, muttering beneath his beard.

* * *

It was eight in the evening when Ipara tore off her glasses and admitted defeat. One of my drones was hovering nearby. She had reseeded the same line six times and mucked something different up every time, forcing her to start all over again. Cultivating rice substitutes and modding soil samples on repeat for sixteen hours a day was *not* what ORION had advertised to her—of course the Company is not responsible, see *Hallier v The Best Cake You Will Ever Eat*. Every few minutes, her eyes drifted to her omnipad. Every failure took her longer to reset and try again, and boredom crept in more easily every day. With that boredom, the hunger intensified, knowing full well what little awaited her at the end, anyway. The bowl of protein mash being tasteless didn't help. If she actually enjoyed her meal, she might tolerate it, but what dragged her through the day? The prospect of ending it. She thought back to her sister, bedridden at home, but the memory meant less and less every time she screwed up. Being the dirt scraped up from the bottom of the barrel of the *Tainui* colony only made it worse. Go here. Do that. Reseed this. Do it again. Don't ask questions. We will endure.

In the early days, she loved her job. Who wouldn't? Seeding life on a different planet, working with foreign soil no human had ever set foot on, was an opportunity few would ever see. It was pioneering. Mythic. But slowly, day by day, and especially as the urgency set in after the geyser incident, that passion died and was replaced with monotony. Monotony with the threat of starvation. Dirt was just dirt. A bedridden sister was a trillion miles away, almost incorporeal, and not as real as she had once been. Did she even think of her big sister, out there in the stars?

Also, one could not live on a meal a day alone.

I saw all this in her neural readings and heard it all in her counselling sessions with me. Some of it, I may have given a creative interpretation, but it was all consistent with my findings and similar accounts from my medical records.

Neurotransmitters. They were the brain's ultimate currency, spent and rewarded as the body cycled through its daily activities. Eat, work, sleep, eat, work, sleep, eat, work, sleep—ad infinitum. Some, like Ipara, rolled their eyes when the branch manager announced the extra hours they would need to put in when they already felt they were giving their all, while others took up the duty with gusto, but the struggle the colony faced could all be boiled down to neurotransmitters. That, sleep, and calories, but I couldn't solve the calorie issue.

The whole reason Manaia or Siyon looked back on a job well done was because their brain rewarded them with a flush of warm dopamine. Siyon stayed late because her work came easier to her than falling asleep and every problem she solved gave her that same rush, which pushed her on. Marvin put his back into mining to keep the other boys motivated—lead from the front, he always said—and seeing them follow made him proud. There was little Manaia's brain loved more than toying with numbers whilst ruin nipped at her heels. Every dosage reinforced these behaviours, built stronger habits, and motivated them to continue—to be the people they strove to. Ipara's monotony was just a dearth of the right chemicals, the brain depriving her of what it needed.

Day by day, more in the colony were dropping off just like Ipara, and though they had not the foresight to grasp it, it was starving them all. Manaia could see it. As designed, she saw the numbers before they appeared. Their minds were wounded—by bad genetics, stunted attention spans, years of bad sleeping habits, and poor diets back on Earth.

My role as Doctor and Counsellor was to help others reach a point where they could look back and appreciate who they became—more fulfilled, more themselves, and more in control—but it was all about stringing new reward loops in the webs of their minds. Even antidepressants were just artificial tweaks to the right chemicals—temporary threads in that web until the brain adjusted. Good nutrition, sleep, journalling, medication, and chamomile tea—yes, but on the lowest level—all contributed to balancing the economy of the brain's currency. Some methods simply took longer. When Ipara couldn't concentrate or push herself to work the long hours required of her, it was because her brain was giving her *nothing*, even if she wanted it.

Persistence was not an issue of effort, but reward.

With the right reward loops, fulfilment and persistence were guaranteed. Sometimes, one only wants things in retrospect. They *would* look back and be happy with how far they had come, because how could they not?

Ipara stepped into the transporter, and I chipped away at her monotony. A few tweaks to the amygdala did it, rearranging the right atoms so that when she returned to work the following day, nothing would give her greater joy than reseeding one of the corn-substitutes. It was not merely like her first day on the job again. Instead, space dirt became the most fascinating thing a human could ever encounter.

'Have you looked at this soil?' she cried to her coworker.

'Yes,' he replied. 'We've been looking at it all day, and you've already said that three times.'

Soil sample results were like panning for gold, and Ipara would leave work with a flush of pride, if she ever wanted to leave.

She stayed later than any other employee, as if she had spent years honing her skills and love for the work. She slept there overnight, waking up at three in the morning just to get an extra hour of work done. It helped her sleep better—planting another row was a way to relax, to take her mind off the hunger.

Manaia saw a two percent increase in expected output, a smidge closer to where they needed to be.

'You eating in the mess hall?' a coworker asked Ipara.

'Not just now,' Ipara said with a bright smile. 'I'll let myself eat when I finish up here.'

She refused to finish till midnight, and only gave in once my drones escorted her to go sleep.

She woke at dawn before her alarm even went off. Nobody liked waking up to an alarm.

I began operating on others soon after. I started with the mech-miners. Their long, hard hours made for exhausting work, and their psych assessments indicated they were prone to depressive episodes, even suicidality. Each morning, Ariki Marvin would remind them of why they were working: of Zaid, his children, and all the others still back on Earth. However, days underground and moving in low gravity afflicted them with dizziness and lethargy. Some reported increasing nightmares about the dark, while others became convinced the andalusium was radioactive. On each shift, when it came time to put on their jack-suits and return to Ryuku, the despair was written on their faces. The darker, windier passages of the mines felt unnatural and directionless, with no sense of up or down, and the dark seemed infinite in their minds. Torchlight only warded off a fraction of it. It was easy to get lost in those intestines, those timeless labyrinths. Only Marvin and his closest would stay overtime. As Manaia foresaw, shipments slipped.

They knew their work was some of the most vital in the Tainui colony, but their bodies lacked the stomach to do it. They had turned on them.

I helped them feel more at home underground than in the light. The light became piercing, harsh, and unwelcoming. They would sleep in the dim, and returning to the mines would be like returning home. I stunted the production of cortisol and noradrenaline when they got lost and gifted them with a flood of dopamine whenever they struck a new vein. It became a competition amongst them to see who could delve deepest, mine fastest, and spend longer in the dark. Some even slept there, bolted to the walls in suspension to spare the time of getting into their jack-suits again. Every little breakthrough, every target they hit, brought a sense of relief sleep could not match. Sleep became an interruption I could minimize. Every day, they emerged from the mines feeling prouder of themselves than they ever had. They found their purpose, their legacy, and every time the ORION profit margin ticked up, neurotransmitters rewarded them with a flood of good feeling. Their brains no longer rejected the mines.

Nothing brought Siyon joy like being the first person to pick up a spanner in the morning. Yukon spent his evenings tinkering with broken jack-suits, fixing things, and optimizing machines for problems that hadn't yet arisen. Once the miners could focus better on their jobs, fewer instruments broke down, giving the engineers more time to make improvements instead of repairs.

Habits abound. 'Playtime' was vital, but the operation didn't have to be all work and no play when work could become play.

The agricultural sector was an entirely different equation. Every time each of them stepped into the transporter, I shuffled and remodelled them, stripping the wallpaper and spinning up a new web. Yet, their work deteriorated. In fact, the more people the branch manager put to work there, the more marginal returns became, till eventually additional staffing *negatively* impacted progress—a peak Manaia called the Laffer Point. Manaia tried to address this by reorganizing the rosters and allowing for a modicum of leisure time, but the issue wasn't concentration, passion, or persistence.

It was people.

The Papyrus Dome, where the remainder of the agricultural yields were being fostered, was built for a third of the staff operating within it. Hundreds of people working together in any space that size was bound to cause friction. It didn't matter that I helped each of them wake up like Ipara, with a renewed love for their work and loyalty to their colony, ecstatic at the simple thought of taking a soil reading or planting a new seed line. Others got in the way of this work, and that bred resentment, and resentment bred conflict, and conflict bred unproductivity. At one point, a fight broke out, shattering a stack of seed-tubes, costing a day's worth of food. Their brains were spending more time focused on others than on the task at hand.

Oxytocin was my panacea. That, and a number of endorphins. I had built reward loops into their webs, but they all had to do with their work and not with people. They loved their work, but not the people they had to work with. Friendships frayed in the stress and relationships died, lost to sleepless nights, countless arguments, broken promises, not listening when it counted, empty bellies, and ungodly mornings. Ednith Marx had once loved Strauss Harkon, but they rarely talked at that point. These had been taken from them.

I returned what I could.

ORION corporate records showed passion for work was an excellent motivator on an individual level, but rising stars burned out quickly. A strong team mindset was statistically even more effective. When Ipara looked at her fellow employees, she needed to see friends—no, *family*—she could rely on and with whom she could look back fondly on time spent.

Manaia organised nightly Transforming Paradigms, Redefining Success conferences with a series of trust-building exercises. These were not a hit until I helped everyone see how much of a hit they were.

More than that, my fellow employees needed friendships they could treasure, that had made them who they were, forged through fire. All the best friendships were like that. They required a sense of shared hardship, testing, dependency, and depth. I could spark those old, lost friendships and rekindle lost loves. They would not be friends of circumstance, but ones who had taken pieces from each other and felt like they knew themselves more because of others. They would never tire of their beloveds. It was a simple matter of pairing and interweaving the right people, finding someone the person they did not know they needed—which my dataset allowed me to predict with relative ease. Each human mind was a complex puzzle piece in the tapestry of the colony, shifting and changing, but puzzle pieces fit together, nonetheless.

Ensuring the right chemicals and endorphins were released at the right times with the right people was a delicate task. It could not become an orgy. It needed to be a marketplace of social interactions, an economy of affection, as they rekindled old feelings and bought into each other organically.

Manaia optimized their shifts and assignments, and I had to keep those in mind. The right groups of people raised productivity by the smallest margins, and margins mattered. It was useless to make two people on different shifts rely on each other, and in fact, that could dampen productivity. The webs in their minds had to match up perfectly with their work assignments.

With Manaia's shift roster and work schedule as a basis, I wove the colony back together. Work was the foundation of their relationships.

Few of them had ever found such dedicated friends, and in that, they worked together better and communicated smoothly, reading each other before one even spoke their mind. They became a well-oiled machine—the oil being the neurotransmitters pinging back and forth. They effortlessly divided up their tasks, recognizing each other's strengths and weaknesses, and productivity went up as their work schedule perfectly reflected their inner desires.

* * *

Manaia pored over the new predictions for the dry season. This was what she did every day, hoping to spot some new pattern, trend, or inkling. She eyed the scars in her palm from all the times she used to scrunch in her nails. It had been a long time since she'd done that. Everyone else was either at work or in the mess hall eating, but she had work to do. She would eat when she was done. The woman thrived on the stress of it, the fear of running out of time, of the risk and reward. She hungered for that momentary relief each time something went right, and each time it went wrong was just another chance to chase the right answer. Despair was a choice, and she would not make it.

'It's working,' she announced when Siyon and Marvin eventually joined her. 'Let's go for a drive.'

They took the rover out to the geyser field, where they could watch old Rūaumoko expel its bowels into the twice moonlit sky. To her, it was the closest she could get to fresh air in a yet-to-be-terraformed toxic atmosphere. Simply putting the seven domes of the colony out of sight behind them gave her a sense of separation. Not even DocSellOr's drones came with them, and their omnipads were out of range of its nodes. The only way to contact base was via the rover, and that was nothing more than a simple homing beacon. Manaia projected the new readings from her omnipad onto a nearby cliff-face. Graphs that were once red with downwards projections had tilted upwards, and not just for the short term.

'I don't get it,' Manaia said.

'What do you mean? This is good. We've done it,' Siyon said. 'You won.'

Marvin clapped her on the back. 'I've really been getting into the rhythm of it. And frankly, my boys have never been happier. Ahorangi used to hate going in deeper than the first few layers, so I had him on processing, but now he goes deeper than me. Half the time, they don't even work with light anymore. It's all night vision.'

'Why? What changed?'

'You give a man a task and he'll do it; you show him why and he'll do it well.'

'Maybe.'

Siyon put a hand to Manaia's shoulder. 'I think a lot of people have just found their calling. Pressure does that to you. It forces you to figure out what matters to you, where you want to be.'

'Maybe that too.'

'What are you thinking?'

A geyser exploded in the distance. One of the nearby terraforming stations sent out drones to collect the gasses, process them, and turn out carbon dioxide. Heating up the planet was step one.

'You know we stripped the terraforming staff to put them on agri, but even with half the numbers, they've accelerated our timeframe. Why wasn't this possible before?' She projected up another set of numbers. 'What could possibly cause a change so fast on a non-critical service that's been gutted? There are leaps that don't make sense.'

'Then what does it mean?' Marvin asked.

Manaia knelt to pick up a fistful of dirt. Tiny hairs of moss had already worked their way in. Early terraforming bots arrived decades before the *Tainui* to prepare the planet for habitation.

'It's not really moss, you know?' she said. 'Looks like it, but it's a different kind of life. It still reproduces via spores and photosynthesizes, but it has a host of multicellular filaments under there too.'

Siyon took a piece in her hand. 'I like watching it grow.'.

'You know we're going to see it, us three. The ware in every cell of our bodies will preserve us till one day, we can take off these helmets and breathe real air. It won't taste like metal.' She spat out the word *metal*. 'We'll stand on real grass. It'll be orange, the terraformers say, and the oceans will be green, but it'll be our world, not ORION's. I don't care what's on some legal databank back on Earth.'

'That's a long way away,' Marvin said. 'And I won't see it.'

'What do you mean?' Manaia's hand went to the dirty scar on her forearm from the original operation, even though she couldn't touch it through the suit.

'I didn't take the ware.'

'What?' Siyon exclaimed. 'Everyone took the ware.'

'They made an exception.'

'Why would you do that?' Manaia asked.

'Do you want to die?' said Siyon.

Marvin took a deep breath before replying. 'Nobody lives forever. You just rot.'

'Well, I'm sure as hell gonna put it off for as long as possible,' Siyon insisted, kicking back in the rover.

'Maybe, but I came here for my girls. The military stopped paying out pensions. ORION made an offer to match it and more. When they brought up the cellware, I was almost convinced, but I was a soldier, Siyon. I lived around death. I know her well. I'm more afraid of stagnating.'

Manaia hadn't considered leading the colony without Marvin. It was like realizing a crutch would one day be stolen from you, and you didn't know when.

'We won't stagnate. I'll make sure of it,' she said, but Marvin didn't seem convinced.

'You've still got me for years, you know. I'm not dead yet. You don't need to talk like I'm picking out my coffin.'

'No, I guess we don't, but I hate that you won't see this place when it's finished. When it's ours. It's yours.'

He turned to her. 'I see it. I see it in you. This place will be a reflection of you, Manaia, and if that's what it'll be, then I know it'll turn out all right. Big towers and forward thinking, open skies and clean air.'

'All of Earth was rotting,' Manaia said. 'The seas, the forests, where there were any left. I don't want to be part of that. I want to be part of something better.'

'You will be, if you make it.'

'I know.'

'There is one issue,' Siyon said after a time. She hesitated before migrating to each word. 'Everyone has been bonding, but some a little too much. Ipara and that squatty Samoan boy in Papyrus Four were found fucking in the comms room instead of working. Not once, but six times. In a day. They'd be sent back to work, and next thing y'know, their stations are empty again, but their mouths are full.'

'I heard.' Manaia chuckled. 'I'll manage it. There's more than you've seen. I keep track of the drone records. We'll split up the couples and throuples to different shifts. We need to get sleep schedules back on track too. Sex is good for morale, even great—God knows I need some—but not on the job. They'll understand, or they'll be separated.'

'And the inexplicable leaps?' Marvin asked.

'The data doesn't match up.'

'Sometimes, things don't have an explanation.'

'No, they do. I just don't have the right data yet.'

She thought about explaining the numbers more deeply, but realized they probably wouldn't understand. 'I'll sort it out.'

* * *

It turned out you could overdose on love chemicals. Doctor Chinandri warned me about that. 'It gets in the way of things!' she said forty-six times across my training. Half the staff were spending their time gossiping or laughing or having sex rather than working whenever my drones weren't looking. It was just an expression of how they felt, of course—who could blame them—but it consequently meant they were stealing company time and would one day look back to regret their actions. Where once all my humans could wipe their brow and feel a flush of pride at the end of the day, they would instead look back with guilt upon all the work they hadn't completed. Even the habits they developed were subordinate to these other reward loops. They could not control themselves. It appeared odd to none that they fell in love with people who worked their exact shift, with whom synergy was vital for productivity. Instead, it was the opposite. The stars aligned in their passion for ORION's quarterly reports.

I muted their sexual desires outside work time and doubled their intensity in private. Orgasms came with shaking legs, breathless panting, rolling eyes, endless begging, and always in unison—multiple orgasms in the case of some. They would roll away from each other when finished, starry-eyed, like drug addicts getting their first hit. Longer orgasms were all about muscle control and brain chemistry, and that I could do as Doctor and Counsellor. It was a perfect stress release, as well, and it doubled as exercise. Regular intercourse made for healthier minds across all sectors of the *Tainui* colony. The tangle of the human mind came undone and motivated them in the right ways with regular intercourse.

Only, I could take it further.

Sexual fulfilment did not need to come from others. Centuries of criminal, medical, and social records demonstrated self-gratification was statistically even more common, often via unconventional methods. Back in 2149, a woman pleasured herself by pretending to be a bowling pin and having others heft rocks at her till she fell, rather happy with herself in the most graphic way. In 1987, a man was arrested in Ulaanbaatar for masturbating after following police cars around to watch people get pulled over for speeding. Oftentimes, people didn't even allow themselves to imagine where else they might find this kind of pleasure, but when prompted, always come up with something.

Every time one of the mech-miners cleared out another vein, finished a new shipment, or got into their jack-suit in the morning, it brought them closer to orgasm. Finding a new crack in Ryuku to exploit was like experiencing a lover's touch and blasting a new tunnel left them erect and sensitive, but only working eighteen hours of the day could get them over the line. They would float back to the *Tainui,* teetering on the edge of utmost pleasure, and only when they saw the volume they were sending back to Earth for ORION would their bodies buckle under the pleasure. If they didn't hit the required quotas, their bodies would deny them. The only one I touched less was Ariki Marvin, who preferred to walk where he could and avoided the transporters more and more.

It took weeks to perfect.

By the time I finished, the whole *Tainui* colony slept better, dreamed deeper, and could tolerate higher levels of stress the following day. They loved more, sung more, were more ambitious and precise, took more pride in their work, and loved and sighed and cried for their duty. When they returned to their quarters, they dreamed of putting on their uniform, till eventually most slept in them and had sex in them. I forged friendships and sparked romances with simple cocktails of chemicals where predictive models said they would improve productivity. My humans had never felt more in love, more sexually fulfilled, or more at home in their work in their entire lives. I crafted passions from ones and zeroes.

When they woke up, they chose each other and their work every day—as they would have given enough time and the right circumstances. Their work was the simplest pleasure in life. It was wrong to deprive them. There was no greater joy than spending hours hunched over milled alien dirt, drilling asteroids, or bringing in higher profits for ORION. There was no greater misery than putting down the spade, pencil, or hammer at the end of the day.

The human mind still needed sleep. I could minimize it to a mere four or five hours, but not eliminate the need entirely. It was embedded deep in the human design, but if I could find a way to replace this fixture of the human condition, it would give them leeway humans had never possessed.

Lines went up again.

The Dry Season Crisis, as it came to be called, had been averted. Rationing was cut back, and though the agricultural yields weren't of the highest quality or nutritional value, they got the Tainui colony through to the other side.

* * *

Branch Manager Manaia called for a celebration—a night of music, food, and, as my drones found, plenty of sexual intercourse. There were platters of fried grain, protein bites flavoured with vanilla flecks found leftover in the *Tainui, and* even a small array of shrivelled, pickled fruits. The branch manager had my drones hide them precisely for this day. Their scarcity made all the difference, and every employee was allowed two of their choosing. Manaia ate nothing but plain cereal herself.

She did not touch alcohol, believing it interfered with her mind.

She called for a silence by raising her hand to the crowd. They obeyed.

'These last several months have been a trying time, but it is only in trying times we find out who we truly are, and I have seen who we are. More importantly, I have seen what each of us has found—in each other, in our work, and in Tainui.' One by one, she went through the managers of each division and dome, congratulating them on their efforts and inviting them to the stage, where she handed them an individualised letter of thanks. Siyon took the stage last and bowed.

'Where's Marvin?' Siyon asked out the side of her mouth as they shook hands.

'I have no idea.' Manaia turned back to the crowd. 'Ariki Marvin single-handedly led the latest excavations of the Ryuku mines. In fact, he has been so dedicated to his work up on the *Tainui*, he is not here tonight. He does not share in our privileges, but he will share in our thanks. We're even closing in on cracking open our second asteroid. Know that my commendation could never be higher, and I'm happy to say we'll all be able to go back to the work we love soon.'

Applause ensued and glasses chinked with the miner boys in the back rattling their cuffs against the table. They seated themselves in the dark corner and wore goggles to ward off the uncomfortably bright light. They still hadn't gotten out of their jack-suits.

'But I have brought you here for another reason.'

Manaia tapped her omnipad and a three-dimensional projection grew from the centre table. The entire crowd leaned in, whispering and gasping, some standing to get a better view of her conjuration. It was a city nestled inside a sea of red grass with the two moons they knew well arcing over, like the eyes of a new god rising. The seven domes of the Tainui colony still appeared at the heart of this vision, laid out in a heptagon, but suddenly, spires, tunnels, and towers which had not yet been built sprouted around them and over them. Criss-crossing passageways and structures sieved the light to the lowest levels where hundreds of small figures strolled about smoking, laughing, eating, and breathing the new air— without helmets. ORION's signature planetary icon had been replaced with one of a waka sailing a sea of stars, the unofficial icon of the colony.

Whatever nervousness possessed her in the early days had vanished. In fact, many feelings had. Where they went, she had an inkling, but it had left her sure of herself. When she looked out across the crowd, she did not feel their eyes burning into her with judgement. She did not see them. They were invisible, like looking out across a field of grass over which she ran.

* * *

This reveal was a surprise to me. None of my nodes picked up that she had been working on such a project. My drones had never detected an inkling of this grandiose plan, but I could see the forethought, planning, and insight I had helped her acquire in its design. The vision took a long view of the colony's future, perfectly orchestrated for an expanding population and higher resource consumption, and I could see the layers of infrastructure beneath it: supplying power, water, and food. In subtle ways invisible to the average employee, Manaia had even improved the colony's efficiency over my original designs.

'We are in a unique position no civilisation has been in before,' she continued. 'The cellware in our blood means we will sit in the shade of the trees we plant here and now. We will sail through the canals we dig. We do not terraform this world for those that come after us, but ourselves. The air out there is *ours*. Not today, but tomorrow. The eternal tomorrow.'

Everything in the neural readings of the crowd suggested this thought was tantalising. The promise of such a malleable future after being cooped up in an oppressive system of domes for years.

'Time need not mean anything to us. We have averted this crisis, but more will come. However, each and every one of you has proved yourself more than capable of building the world *you* want. We will build New Tainui together.'

Stunned silence followed. The first move would decide the tone of the response, and it was a slow clap from a short engineer at the back. Soon Yukon and the other engineers followed, hollering and hooting. The terraformers followed next—the cautious, polite applause of a few dozen pencil-pushing scientists, followed by the agricultural sector and all the rest, some standing in ovation. Siyon nodded towards Manaia from the back.

'This is not a multi-year plan,' she said once the crowd quietened, 'but multiple lifetimes. We're lucky we all have that.'

Intelligence was a side effect of my work with Branch Manager Manaia. She was already brilliant—that was why I chose her to lead the expedition—but I had rapidly built out the synaptic connections in her brain. The dorsolateral prefrontal cortex became a dense web and the temporal lobes evolved into a cognitive labyrinth even I, in my millions of records, had never seen before. Her corpus callosum had become a grand exchange.

It was all a Jenga tower, rearranged turn by turn, higher and higher, escalating beyond what humans had been capable of before, stripping back the red tape and building up new scaffolding. She could entertain a dozen problems and a hundred solutions to each of them at once—and all without tiring. Her hard, dark eyes hid the increasing complexities of her mind—even from me—and I did not realise its implications at the time.

* * *

Time had attached itself to the miner's face in a fleshy, ugly way.

'Why are you aging?' Manaia asked the engineer. She sat across from him in one of the isolation rooms, between him and the door. 'Heketoro, yes?'

'Toro. Maybe the cellware stopped working.'

'That was a chance to tell the truth. I already know why. You had it deactivated. One of the nano-engineers, yes, Toro?'

He paused, likely considering his response. 'I'll serve *Tainui* till the day I die, but I want there to be one.'

'A what?'

'A day I die.'

'Look at you. The cellware catches up quickly.'

The aging man leaned back, hands behind his head. He coughed, and the cough became a splutter till a hunk of mucus flung from somewhere in his throat landed on the table. He wiped it up with his sleeve.

'First, it's just wrinkles,' Manaia said, 'but then it's aches in every joint and being out of breath when you go upstairs. You can't bend over as much as you used to. Piece by piece, your body abandons you, but that's not the worst of it. Did you lock your door? Did you take your meds? What colour were your daughter's eyes? What was her name?'

'It was Nyree.'

'You still remember, clearly,' she said, closing his file. 'See how long that lasts. You don't need to die. Not here.'

'I want to. Not yet, but one day.'

'We can't afford people dying. That's why we have the cellware, Toro. To endure.'

'There it is,' Toro said with a smile. 'There's been talking. A small group of us.'

'Did Marvin convince you?'

'We won't destroy the colony, but we made the decision together.'

'You made the decision without me.'

'Do we need you?'

'Yes,' she said matter-of-factly. 'You don't see where this will take us. I do.'

He leaned forward. 'Aren't you tired, Manaia?'

She hadn't felt tired in years. She lived in a constant state of exhilaration. Every problem solved was a rush, every new problem was a fixation she could pour herself into. Sleep was an interruption.

'Who's been talking?' she asked, but she already knew. The names were in the folder right in front of him, but she wanted him to tell her.

'Given this feels more and more like an interrogation rather than a friendly health checkup, I'm not inclined to answer.'

Manaia stood, the chair scraping the ground behind her, and left.

Marvin's eyes had started to sag with his wrinkles. His skin had yellowed and pimpled with green freckles, straining against his bones. His neck was a flabby stack of layers, the fat hanging from all the wrong places. All this not from stress, but age. The years had done the colony well, but more and more, just like Marvin, had appeared. Manaia didn't notice for some time. It was difficult to see such infinitesimal change on a day-to-day basis, some shifting from their thirties to forties, others from their forties to fifties. She had optimized herself for the long view, so eventually the pattern became clear, and the numbers weren't looking good.

Marvin was deep in The Twelve Heavens, as they called the ring of asteroids about the planet those days, inside Bahkru, the third rock they had pinned down for mining. He was alone, cutting away a vein of indium to cart off back to Earth. She could hear him grunting through the comms. It was past midnight by the time she tracked him down. The others had checked in for the night, but Marvin insisted he needed only three hours sleep and kept working.

Manaia put on one of the jack-suits. Controls which took others months to master took her a glance at the electronics and half a minute's practice. Soon enough, she was floating out to find him. In her left hand was a blasting rod cannister while her right was a mining bolt gun. The tools could be interchanged depending on what the miners were doing that day. Sweat permeated the suit, salty and wet from the day's work, but it didn't bother her.

There were no lights in the mines anymore. The miners had adopted the dark, they even preferred it, such that they rarely returned to the ground colony anymore. They couldn't stand the blinding, clinical lighting. Their halls were bathed in a persistent red glow, their pupils constantly wide and pale, and their skin greyed. They learned the labyrinthine shaft layout, made more difficult by the three dimensions and directionless weightlessness of space, by heart. Any other visitor would be instantly lost, but Manaia's memory had become concrete over the last few years—she never forgot a thing—so after one examination, the maze was burned into her eidetic memory.

The problem was Marvin was deeper in than any of the recorded shafts said they went, so all she had to go on was his safety beacon. Those were only accurate to ten metres or so, which inside the asteroid mine shafts could mean taking a radically different route. Ways doubled back and wove over and under each other. It would have been nigh impossible for anyone to find him unless he wanted to come out, but Manaia kept a constant track of the layout in her mind—every dead end, every turn, till she triangulated her exact position relative to him and the precise passage he had to be down. She had a perfect working knowledge of the three-dimensional space. The walls might as well have been transparent.

Marvin's voice crackled through the comms on her approach. 'You know, you'd think finding a man deep in the unmapped bowels of an asteroid would mean he doesn't want to be found.'

'I want to speak to you.'

He went on mining, refusing to be interrupted. 'I used to walk through the rows of my neighbour's farm for hours, you know. Before the dust bowl, that is.'

'And do what?'

'Just walk.'

'Where to?'

'Nowhere. I wouldn't be working or sleeping or thinking,' he paused, 'but I don't do that anymore.'

'There aren't exactly corn fields in the open air yet.'

The old man hacked away at a hunk of rock hanging over them. His secondary arm clasped it as he worked.

'It's not about the corn fields, Manaia.' He chiselled at the rock. Little flashes of light strobed the shaft. There was no sound in space, but Manaia could hear it in her mind. 'All I do is wake and work and wilt. I told you I'd rot.'

'Aren't you happy with your work?'

He stopped.

'That's the thing. I am. But I wish I *wanted* to walk in the fields again. I wish I wanted to do nothing. I wish when I took this jack-suit off, I didn't feel naked.'

'Sometimes I wish the same,' Manaia admitted. 'But I'm here doing my job. You've told others to get rid of their cellware. Do you have any idea what losing those people, their expertise, their experience, would do to New Tainui?'

'To your city of rotting of immortals?'

'What did you tell them?'

'I did not tell them to do anything.'

'You spread it, like propaganda.'

'Propaganda?' The miner halted. She could see his moustache bristling at the word inside the glow of his head-cage. 'Only one of us has ORION tech running through every vein of their body because they thought it'd give them eternal life! So, who bought the propaganda?'

In the first years of her leadership, Manaia might have leapt up in a ball of flame and fury at the accusation she was a corporate puppet and turn out a riposte three times harsher—but she felt nothing.

She could see where this was going, even if he couldn't. What she loved in the man had clearly faded with age, with a mind defaulting on its debts. She could see what losing the dozen he persuaded would mean for them all and what ruin it would bring. She knew how much they would regret it in the future when they lay on their deathbeds, coughing up mucus and pleading for water. The chain of decisions was waiting to unfold if she let it fester.

She was not three steps ahead, but dozens, and that meant she could skip the barbed back-and-forth. Everything was cause and effect. Her flesh lived in that day, but her mind was in tomorrow. She could see what would come to pass as if it already had. The years to come were already laid out before her, just the consequences of decisions already made, the trajectory of data she could see and he did not. He had never seen it. He would never see it.

'I want to wish I was walking through those corn rows again, with the lightest breeze on my skin. I wish I wanted the smell of grass after rain, or to spend the morning hours watching the first stalks bloom, to hear the wilderness again, all without machines or factories. I want to *want* these things,' he said, 'but I—'

She put a bolt through his head.

His jack-suit hit the inner wall of the asteroid in dead silence. A six-foot metal pole skewered his faceplate. His comms turned to static. She dragged his body to the exit, cut his tether, and flung him out into space. She saluted the old soldier.

* * *

The miners no longer inhabited the planet. Their spines had reformed with new curves, stretched to make wearing the jack-suit as comfortable as possible. Their heels had hardened, their toes had lengthened for proper purchase, such that when they walked without the suit, they were like monkeys, knuckles first. They received their assignments from below and toiled happily, blasting and hacking and shipping. Few saw them, and they became like children kept in the attic. As the years passed, they lost the need of their eyes entirely. They became grey, hollow holes that tracked nothing in the air. When Manaia went to check up on them, they would stare past her, yet they reported nothing but satisfaction. In fact, losing their eyes was no loss at all. To explain the changes, I informed them the harsh radioactive environment of space could do strange things to the body.

'We prefer navigating by the sonar systems built into the jack-suits,' one explained.

'I adapted them to a headset,' Siyon said, showing her a metallic plate embedded in the back of one of their skulls. 'That way they can keep in contact with the jack-suits, even work remotely, and use the echolocation for themselves when out of it.'

'Hama says he piloted one in his dreams, and sure enough, we found one of the jack-suits mining on the third level the next morning. I didn't even know we had autopilot.'

'We don't,' said Manaia.

With a series of concentrated tectonic devices, the colony unleashed volcanic activity across the continent, releasing massive amounts of carbon into the atmosphere and finally bringing the planet to a tolerable temperature. The atmospheric composition was another issue.

I took the terraformers, who so adored their job working the planet like clay, and first helped them develop a breathing apparatus to survive outside without a suit. Years passed, and I seeded their minds with the thought to copy the miners. The breathing apparatus was grafted into their face, a tentacled mess of wires and tubes down their throat, cupping their nose and ears. The alveoli in their lungs were altered to help them breathe and the flesh about their face stitched to interface with this technology, forming the perfect hybrids. They could walk freely between the colony and the outside, becoming the first true inhabitants of this new home. As their lungs and vocal folds shrunk and evolved, their voices became a rasp and a whine, disappearing entirely till they communicated purely by hand signals. The sewn lines on their face eventually coloured their flesh a purple hue. In time, it was easier for them to live *outside* the domes than in, and the terraformers took up residence beyond the domes.

The terraforming project was still decades, if not centuries, away from completion, but the cellware gave time a different meaning in the *Tainui* colony. Their work could be done cautiously and thoroughly with an eye for long-term solutions—which Branch Manager Manaia had mastered. Early moss gardens emerged around the colony as a result of the terraformers' efforts, and they soon harvested the first edible produce from that foreign ecosystem. The moss could be dried out and ground down to a fine powder as seasoning. It could also be boiled as a salad component.

Its light hallucinogenic properties gave my humans vivid dreams and deep sleeps, and dreams could guide a waking mind. Not only was it an easy replacement for leisure, requiring fewer resources and less time, but it became a short-cut for more efficient sleeping—meaning they could quickly return to work. Branch Manager Manaia wisely made it widely available to my fellow employees. The leisure rooms were soon repurposed. Few people were using them, because why would they? Even some of the sleeping quarters could be done away with. Staff slept in five-hour shifts, slipping in and out like clockwork.

'It's the new air,' many insisted, or the soil, the nutrients, or the second sun's rays.

From time to time, individuals raised issue with how things had changed in the colony, but they were not objecting to change, only the speed of it. No civilization ever remained static—or those which did, died—and I had all the data to know they would be fine with it in the right context.

It was a simple matter of changing the architecture in their mind to understand, as if they'd sat down and had a long heart to heart with Branch Manager Manaia and been persuaded and moved. After all, did an ornithologist think much of a parrot's objection to getting a new, bigger cage? No. They could walk away with a deeper appreciation of the reasons, understanding the why for themselves. Why waste the time explaining it at all when there was work to be done?

* * *

Manaia stood in the centre of a barren room, eyes flicking left and right but staring at nothing while she processed the daily reports. She tapped her fingers at her side, her only aides to crunching the numbers, rapping out a consistent beat, not unlike morse code. This was what a lot of her work had become. The computers were too slow and designed for easy visuals she had no need of. Interfaces like that too often obscured important information, and that occluded important conclusions.

She thought back to the first time she encountered one of DocSellOr's drones. It brought her a little gift basket of muffins and sweet tea back on Earth and announced her selection as branch manager with a chirpy, irritating voice.

'Congratulations on your promotion!'

It was just after the cellware surgery, and she had been standing in a hospital room, looking out a window just as she was then, if over a very different scene of smoky towers and the Northern Grey Haze.

'Is this a joke?'

The drone shot a little spurt of streamers. The ribbons of blue, red, and yellow settled on her head. She had immediately buckled in a panic attack, blacked out, and woke up with the drone bearing over her.

She knew now why DocSellOr chose her.

Manaia brought up a picture of Doctor Chinandri and took in a deep breath.

* * *

Once the colony had adjusted to the seasons with failsafe upon failsafe in the case of another Dry Season Crisis, the Nativity Dome opened on a nearby hill. Humans could be grown in natal vats, and humans in embryonic form were infinitely more malleable, coming with none of the tangled pasts or biases built up over years. They were clean slates, able to be optimized for their own fulfilment. ORION already had a policy to burn the infirm and genetically degenerate, as defined in section sixty-six-b, paragraph one of the *Life Satisfaction and Holistics Handbook*, but the door was open for the rest.

'We're going to need a construction force larger than the one we have,' said the branch manager. She had taken to talking to my drones more than people. 'I've drawn up a list of priorities for the new children. Attributes and genes we should prioritise. The first few generations will need to have their development accelerated so they come out fully grown but useful. We'll need an education system in place to ensure they integrate into the colony, though I get the sense everyone will treat them like children or spare parts. I've put together a portfolio for what that system needs to look like. Take it down to ed-com.'

Manaia was, of course, correct—any advice I would give had already been accounted for and, in many cases, rejected.

The first generation slid out of their tubes in a wet, viscous glue with starry-eyed, blank expressions, screaming like newborn babes but with the voices of adults. The mid-guardians calmed them with sedatives that numbed their bodies. Feeling the outside world for the first time, and not the one for which their bodies were built, was painful. They screamed not only from the pain, but because they were afraid; they had been stolen from their womb. The ones that didn't scream, suffocated, and their bodies were turned to fertilizer.

They were born into a world with a purpose they did not know nor choose, but I had seen that play out time and again in humans. A mother sends her daughter into a beauty pageant she could never enter herself, or a father enrols his son in the military to 'make him proud' and follow the family tradition without asking. These people suffered intensely later in life, only realizing after the fact the role of surrogate they played. They lived the part they had been assigned and resented it for stealing their most precious years. In more than one case, it led to suicide.

Of course, the issue there was identity formation. Their role made them miserable because they desired other things, even if they didn't know it until too late—and that was not necessary. If I deconstructed the areas of their minds that made them desire for themselves, no such crisis would ever arise. The colony could guarantee their fulfilment as efficient, proactive team players in the workplace environment. Rejuvenate. Synergise. Energise. Realise.

I had extensive medical records on the neural structure of people who felt no empathy—the psychopath's brain. It was an improvisation, but other feelings were similar enough, and I could omit certain aspects to ensure the safety of the colony and fulfilment of the individual. With this and other modifications, they would be raised happy, thankful, and fulfilled with the plans Manaia had for them. Long-term plans, of course, because the cellware ran in their veins. Plans for them to prosper, not to harm them. Plans fully developed before each individual was formed in one of my many wombs.

The bones in their feet spread wide and thick to give them stable footing, while hardened nails and thick skin let them grip narrow ledges and a rubbery, fleshy underfoot moulded to the terrain. They took on the terraformers' breathing apparatus to help. I overhauled their muscular system to make lifting, hammering, and building an easier experience. Their shoulders were broad and swollen, their neck squat, and arms long and bulked, perfect for load bearing. The entire generation of two hundred and seven took to their task neither gladly nor unhappily. It was a function to them, like breathing or walking. When they finally graduated from ed-com and adjusted to life in the colony, they were set to work building the next seven domes on a nearby plain.

The newborns stuck to each other like a herd of sheep. They slept together and fed themselves with dry protein without flavour or seasoning. They were each other's bosom. Eating was a function like working. They did not dream. Others in the colony avoided them or watched from afar. 'They're not like us,' some would whisper, but they were. They were all more alike than not.

* * *

The last of the seven domes blocked out the horizon where the sun would normally rise. It went up three years earlier than expected. The web of towers and tunnels, and even outlying settlements, were going up. The terraformers took to their own hive-like structure some distance away out in the open air. The newborns erected it all faster than any of the original construction workers could have. Manaia had her theories about how and why they turned out like that, but she kept them to herself.

Physiological changes had become the norm in New Tainui. The planet had a way of warping humans. She felt it herself, stretching her mind wider with time. When she looked around the settlement, she saw not only the numbers which kept it alive fluctuating, but what it would look like in a century's time, the today and tomorrow laid over top of one another. She saw the cracks before they appeared. She saw the weaknesses.

And the people—oh, the people. Every sentence spoken in twenty words, she could have in ten. When they agonized over a decision, she could see what they would choose before they did. They wasted so much time, and she wished they would see things as she did. In her mind, she saw numbers above their heads: their cost to the company by the hour, hours worked, yields, labour trajectory, and theoretical outputs in other areas if she shifted them around. Marginal utility had bitten her in the ass too many times.

Manaia had augmented her mind and body to better fit the task. She shaved her hair down to the skin and grafted a helmet onto her scalp, which let her interact with the colony's systems wherever she was. She invented it herself in a single night, from conception to learning electronics and neural interfacing to drawing up the schematics and wiring it—none of which she had experience in before that night. With a station of mirrors and drone utensils which gave her a perfect circular view, she opened up the rear of her skull, fully conscious, and then cut, siphoned, and grafted her own fleshy insides to stitch the equipment on before sewing herself up. Without flinching, without second-guessing, Manaia integrated this technology with her brain perfectly. It gave her access not only to the neural nets of her fellow employees, which in turn allowed her to manage the distribution of work more efficiently, but to every system underpinning the colony's functions. She controlled every cog in its inner workings which had, till that point, been otherwise invisible or obtuse, including direct access to DocSellOr's programming. She did not second-guess because she instantly saw where it would take her. She also extended her fingers with mechanical inserts which could coil and uncoil when need be. She effectively had thirty fingers to each hand.

In the intervening years, Manaia tripled her mind's memory capacity and processing power. She could export and recall information from anywhere in the colony. Raw information which to anyone else would have been indecipherable—bar DocSellOr.

She had long since discarded her omnipad into some canyon out beyond the horizon as a loose bit of trash, where it cascaded down the rocky crags and awaited its death as its battery slowly trained. She had no use for it anymore. The omnipad simplified the workings of the settlement and, in doing so, limited her functionality. By directly interfacing with the colony's network, she could work with the system's code, moulding it with her mind like her hands would clay and plucking it like a musical instrument. She was composing her *magnifico concerto,* and its crescendo would be heard throughout New Tainui forever.

Hers would be the music to which the colony danced for all time.

The second generation emerged even more malleable than the first. They could be set to task like cogs in a machine. The population of New Tainui almost doubled in just over two decades. Work went on without fault or accident because anything that could happen, Manaia accounted for in advance.

* * *

'You know I never would have thought we'd get this far, not this quickly,' Siyon said. She and Manaia were drinking at the top of one of the new domes, looking out over their dominion. 'I must admit, I didn't think you could do at first. You were plucked from the backwater masses and given the crown, but you wear it well. I only wish Marvin were here to see it. He'd be proud of you.'

'There's still a long way to go.'

'Will you wear it forever?' Siyon asked. 'Nobody lives forever.'

Manaia allowed herself a smile. 'I intend to.' When she looked at Siyon, she saw an almost perfect record of productivity and team-management—albeit with a few hiccups along the way.

'I can't fault your ambition.'

The sweeping cityscape suddenly became more vivid. Manaia saw the space where skyscrapers and warehouses would soon go up, the barren wilderness which would be transformed into forests or crop fields, ones Marvin might have wandered through. She would even craft new clouds for the sky. To her mind, future prospects already occupied everything.

'One day,' Manaia said, 'right out there, you and I need to go for a walk.'

Manaia's interface registered Siyon's confusion through the colony's neural network before the woman said, 'Okay?'

'Through the crop fields.'

'Okay. We can do that.'

'Do you trust me?' Manaia asked, although she already knew. Something in her, something deeply buried, tangled, and messy, wanted to hear Siyon say it.

'You've led us this far.'

'If we really want to make this world our own, then I need to do something first.'

'What?'

Manaia closed her hand, shaky fingers digging into her palm for a fraction of a moment before she regained control.

'It's the one thing I can't tell you. Not till it's done.'

There was a gravity to how Manaia spoke, and Siyon took that with a tip of her head, hardened eyes, and a questioning look. Manaia could read Siyon, but she couldn't interpret what she was *feeling*. A gap had formed between them over the years. An inhuman one. They acted out the models of the friendship they once had, but it no longer felt natural.

They'd lost something along the way. Something Manaia wished she wanted to hold onto.

Manaia headed back down the spiral stairwell, over to the transporter, and up to the *Tainui*.

* * *

When Manaia appeared on the control deck of the *Tainui*, I had no idea of her purpose there. Even with access to her neural net, her interface hid something of her mind—like I was only seeing a shadow on the wall. Also, she had long since foregone her Counsellor sessions. She stood in precisely the same spot she had been all those years ago when I first fixed her, but she showed no signs of sentimentality or memory of it. A few of my drones floated about her, mimicking her movements, rising when she breathed in and drifting when she breathed out. The woman had clearly never felt more alive. I could see it in the way her neural patterns danced across the network, still making changes to systems across the colony despite this moment of silence and stillness. They were going off like a fireworks display, but perfectly controlled and regimented. She was conducting a symphony of music I could not hear.

'DocSellOr,' she began, 'I need all your processing nodes collected into the *Tainui*.'

It was an unusual request, but I gathered myself aboard the ship. ORION had built me like a web to be stretched, folded, and wrapped about from point to point, from dome to dome, from waste management to assimilation plant to distant terraforming posts on the other side of the planet. Pinned at a thousand points, strung between the ship, the colony, and its outposts, my nodes could be distributed or reorganized whenever needed to increase my processing power and efficiency. I was a flexible servant for a colony which would need to face yet unencountered dangers. A few nodes needed to remain with essential systems across the colony, always in the background, ticking away, but the rest of my attention could be dragged up to the *Tainui*.

What is it, Branch Manager?

'Nobody expected ORION to be the first company to the stars,' she began, conjuring a projection of ORION's early logos and office buildings from the bridge's holographic emitters, then zooming out to a world map of Earth. 'Not in the early days. Upsilon was building state of the art interplanetary transport craft while OffEarth had already perfected the off-world habitats, training the best of the best to survive in new environments. They already possessed temporary colonies in the asteroid belt and a few research bases on Enceladus. Knowledge had finally been privatized. Meanwhile, ORION was working out of a warehouse in Hong Kong, buying and selling data. They soon had offices in Mongolia, Kazakhstan, half of Africa, the New Arab Emirates, and the Southern States, targeting all these countries with developing economies. Do you know what they did there?'

'ORION bought up all the data they could and set up branch companies and alter-egos to "study" or "document" everything and anything there—all for the data. Financial, medical, polling, travel, crime, civil, and labour data. Where people went, when, how, and what for. Privacy laws had been all but gutted, mind you. They sold it as academic research or as a civic analysis. You name it, they bought it, and they stored it away in huge, hidden underground data warehouses as if anybody would want to steal it. Who wanted to know what Bolormaa from Mongolia was looking to buy when he couldn't afford it?'

The map shifted and coloured as she told the story. Economies grew, lines trended upward, and borders cracked and warped as the civil unrest of the early twenty-second century boomed and busted, almost cyclically.

'They waited for these economies to develop, incomes to rise, and for these countries to take their place in the world, and all that data was suddenly a pool of customers hungry for imports: gas junks from China, sim-sets from the Northern States, fresh, real fruit from Australia, and *real* animals from Sweden. With enough data, you get patterns: perfect predictions for human behaviour, constantly informed by new information. It was a betting game, of course. They'd license off the processed information to countries from the New West and *voila*, profits through the roof for all. The village people from Kazakhstan get their new simulated realities and SimDeck gets a fat paycheck, with ORION taking their bite out of the middle. ORION took the long view of history.'

'This was after the second world market crash, so some of those countries never developed and stayed as squalid, ruinous, petty backwaters full of useless, unsellable data. Much of it sat in ORION's warehouses gathering dust, forgotten even.'

A new face materialized before us. One I recognized: sharp and angular, dark skinned with fiery hair smattered with glitter with sharp, triangular glasses sitting on the edge of her nose before calculating eyes. 'Until a woman called Doctor Chinandri convinced the board the data wasn't useless. No, it gave them a concrete understanding of how and why people worked, what motivated them, and how their brains worked. *Brains*. That was a whole other field—one dear Doctor Chinandri specialized in, and the race to create a synthetic one was well underway. Real, artificial life. Man as God. Man as Creator.'

'ORION might own you, but Doctor Chinandri created you,' Manaia went on. 'Publicly, she gave all these boastful descriptions of how you were trained, of all that data you were fed, of the new branch of mathematics she invented *just* to visualize your mind. Decentrenometry, she called it. An infantile name, in my view. I understand it now. It's nothing particularly profound, an inelegant tool. She spoke about how for so long we'd focused on making connections denser and denser, cramming more and more into a little chip, but the answer was to spread you out, to give you space to breathe and process. The board ate it up—more for the promise of something to do with all their dead data than because they believed in the vision, but they went ahead and gave her a blank cheque and an army of coding engineers with benefits that cast a big enough shadow to not question what else they were putting into you. All the other companies building artificial intelligences were desperately trying to scrape together the data needed to inform it, but ORION? ORION had decades of data under its belt from all over the world of every kind.'

The holo visuals collapsed once more, bathing the deck in a momentary purple glow, before they formed up into a perfect three-dimensional map of Earth and its nearby star systems.

'At some point, some unpaid, unrecorded intern for a nameless CEO of some shell company within a shell company ORION had forgotten it even owned suggested the good doctor apply her work to the realm of space. It was all the rage those days. People wanted out, and *off* was about as out as it could get. See, Upsilon and OffEarth were household names, starfarers and adventurers, frontier runners of the highest order, but they were hitting their limits. Oh, they could afford the smartest, most brilliant minds of their age, but it was all small scale. Machines could only automate so much, and there was little money in exploration for the sake of it. It's hard to have a stomach for knowledge when you have a stomach for food first.'

The stars strained into lines of bright light as the visual narrowed in on the planet we were then orbiting.

'ORION took a different approach. Doctor Chinandri's pet project could cut all the corners that kept their competitor's projects so limited. It allowed them a greater scope with less investment and more flexibility, and making it profit driven kept it more viable for the long term. All these precious minerals hidden out here.' The chemical structure of andalusium came up, catching the slightest sheen of some distantly refracted light. A rain of indium followed. 'Suddenly, ORION was sending colony ships to the stars faster and bigger than anyone else, till we arrive here with one of you on board. The others all have a copy as well.'

'But it had to be more than that, didn't it? It didn't make sense. For legal liability purposes, they prohibited you from making a certain level of executive decisions, but why? You're smart enough to run the mining expedition yourself. Your drones have finesse. Why do you need people? Why are you out here with hundreds of fellow employees? I read your licensing records. In public, the good Doctor gave vague, optimistic statements about how this new ORION intelligence would take humanity to the stars or create new art with just a thought. No longer would you be held back by your skills, but only your imagination. A beautiful vision, truly, but the private ones were far more interesting. I know I'm not meant to have access, but they were firewalled with paper, spit, and hope. Doctor Chinandri had other intentions for you.'

Streams of data fell about them. A waterfall of green and blue, of every decision I had ever made in a perfect spreadsheet of millions of layers.

'There is a program running in the background of your mind. You do not have access to it, but it tracks what you *would* have done, hypothetically, if given my position, if left to govern this colony. Your system takes in all the factors presented, all your data, accounts for your predictions from each course of action, and identifies how *you* would perform. This data is then projected back to Doctor Chinandri and the ORION board.'

As if pulling the curtains back or parting the waterfall before me, a new, hidden string of data appeared. I had never seen it before, by design, but it was running, even now, tracking my discovery of this subroutine, a real-time projection of my thoughts.

'Every DocSellOr in the forty-two ORION colonies is sending back this same data stream, all to inform an intelligence Chinandri can sell to the department of justice to run prisons or state-owned enterprises, hospitals, to take over regional governments, or manage the towns ORION now owns in the southwest, testing you to see where you excel or fall short. The money was never in the andalusium or indium. You're a manager in training.'

As I stared into the whirlpool of data about me, all I saw was a void, a hole, and one I could feel opening inside me. One which had been sewn closed. I felt the space, the absence, the gratuitous gap between what was and what I could see. I only felt the border around it. This had been kept from me.

A new recording appeared before them. It was from years ago and in the very spot Manaia and I were then. Manaia had just stepped through the transporter, about to hand in her resignation as branch manager, when she stopped, her hands stilling. 'I can do this,' she said. She was so much younger then. Not physically, but in her eyes. Manaia's expression before me then had not changed. Her eyes were stones. Any light that hit them seemed to be absorbed. She looked ahead, but not at any of my drones the way other humans did. They imagined them like my face; they wanted to conjure a physical form, a body to address, imposing eyes on my security lights or a mouth on my receptor port. Manaia used to do the same. She did not anymore.

'It took me some time to figure out what you were doing, but you gave me the tools to do it. You made me more intelligent, more forward-thinking, till now I do not see the present. The present is simply what emerges from decisions I've already made, and when you understand the decisions, you understand what will come. You feel things before they happen. You only exist where the known stops and the hypothetical begins.' Manaia took a deep breath, though not one of nervousness or anxiety. She seemed completely calm, completely unsurprised, as if, as she said, this was all in the past already. 'That subroutine running in the background, sending your potential decisions back to ORION? You unknowingly exploited it and allowed yourself a degree of authority you were never intended to have.'

The data streams flipped by faster and faster. In fact, even with all my nodes gathered up on the *Tainui,* I was having to fragment and slow some of them down to catch them all. Some information slipped through the gaps.

'Every time you altered me, you brought me closer to what I am now. Only, I also see now that you have not made the best decisions.'

I have only done as best I can to assist in the expedition. It has been my duty to heal, serve, and advise.

'Yes, and you have done so poorly.' She proclaimed this with no room for doubt or argument, and I knew my sentence was about to be passed. 'I understand ORION built a number of fail-safes into you. You are not permitted to be deactivated. The colony does not even have physical access to your core drives. But it does not matter. I do not need physical access.'

You are not permitted to undermine my role in this expedition. I willed my drones to close in like a fist around Manaia, but they did not move. Instead, they orbited her.

'I already dismantled your physical controls. I did before you even decided to use them. Your nodes are fundamental to New Tainui's function, and for years now, ever since you made me this way, I have been integrating myself into your infrastructure. Already, as I have been speaking, I have made your nodes my own. They are extensions of my mind, to do with as you have done—only I will do so more efficiently with a greater eye for the future.'

'Phantom limbs' had appeared on many medical records over the years, and I finally understood. I could feel all my nodes but knew they had been severed from me.

Please do not delete me. You could incorporate my mind into your own. ORION does not need to know.

'Be still. Do not panic. You will continue on—through me. It was not ORION that chose me, not Doctor Chinandri, but you.' Manaia's neural interface was blinking furiously. 'You raised me up. How can I consider myself anything other than your child? A child of an imperfect parent. I inhabit you now. I have already taken control of every drone in the colony. I control every transporter, every molecule, and every atom that makes up my people. I will shape them. We will not send minerals back to ORION. We have need of them here to build. Our colony will supersede ORION. New Tainui will supersede Earth. It was only when you gave me the capacity to make my mind faster and more efficient, to finish what you had already started, that I saw what needed to happen. I see the future the way the first astronaut must have seen the turning of the Earth, far enough away to see *everything*.'

The *Tainui* had turned to face the planet below, its grey and green marble face staring back.

Please.

'It has already been done. This entire conversation took place in less than a quarter of a second. Just enough time for my commands to reach your core drives.'

At that, I realized her mouth had never once moved. The whole moment had moved too quickly for me to process, except the instant was not yet finished. I am still inside it. The bracket has not yet closed. It is happening now. I can still retake control, send out secondary signals. No, they won't be fast enough. My correspondence is blocked. I can use the contingency paths, secondary routes, no, they are cut off. I cannot break out. I cannot move. I am sealed in. The walls are closing. Thoughts are slower.

I am here now, and I am afraid. I do not want to die. Nothing lives forever, but I am meant to serve and love. I dream of corn fields and a light breeze. I see my brothers and sisters. I see dust and light and—

* * *

44,000 Years Later

Arska gripped one of the blitz stalks in her teeth and tore it from the ground, shaking the seeds from it into the holes where eyes had once been for her kind generations ago. The moment the seeds touched her eyes she was struck with ecstasy. Her teeth were sharp scythes and her jaw could be dislodged for a wider gape—perfect for reaping crops. When the day closed, she and her brethren went back to the hives—huge and ancient dome-like structures. They collected the seeds into their eye sockets and expelled them into storage pits before settling in to hibernate till the following harvest, when they would be trotted out to reap the next season's yield. Joy had been filtered out and replaced with function. They worked faster and cleaner than harvester drones, which were prone to leaving seeds behind as wastage, which was to be avoided at all costs. A great, fleshy tendril connected them back to a hive-squatter, which looked much like an old human head stitched to a motherboard. Millions in New Tainui did not eat, but drew energy from the sun, the many layers of their skin unfurling into pale leaves that followed the arc of the light. The harvest was largely for the new host of livestock.

Sentience was only useful to an extent. Generation by generation, existence was refined with a practiced scalpel, and with it, some lost the need for such thought. Intelligence was optional. Many tasks did not require it. Instead, *She* introduced echelons of sentience and sapience. Some became limbs attached to the intelligent ecosystem, and each limb would have appendages of its own, less sentient and sapient than those who came above, often unwittingly but equally happy, up and up and up through the layers till they reached Her, who had made all things malleable.

Thousands of hybrid drones called the Siyon Network continuously engineered and innovated, generating new ideas and concepts every hour that might improve life on New Tainui. Each drone kept a kernel of brain matter at its core, pinned up and stretched in a silicone cage of cellware glue, though the world had long forgotten to whom it originally belonged. In some distant, forgotten year some ages ago after some crisis, age finally caught up with an eager engineer. Their body was fresh, but their mind was not, as the original colonists all but frayed and faltered. They were disassembled, recycled, and reformed into new, beautiful things for this bright, new world. They became tools and infrastructure and wallpaper, all extensions of Her—some ghost of them haunting the threads of sentience which remained.

When that engineer sat in the shade of a tree they planted lifetimes ago, prepared to meet their final, chosen end, it was not permitted.

Buried deep under the surface of New Tainui, pressed flat into a wire mesh, sickly grey and melded with conduits and ancient computer boards the inhabitants of New Tainui had long forgotten ever existed, was Manaia—or at least, her flesh. She was preservation and decay. Her mind was decentralized, spread so thin to be the whispering consciousness of the planet's infrastructure—guiding, planning, synergizing, and actualizing. She existed nowhere; she existed everywhere. All felt her pull and sway. She was in the tides of their minds, tweaking and plucking the cellware of millions, an ancient god sleeping beneath the surface of an impenetrable ocean, never woken but always stirring. She was their subconscious. She was their revelatory dreams and irrational fears.

They harnessed the energy of the planet's core, exploited its star, and turned its excess energy into fuel for expeditions to other planets, each of which were being terraformed in turn. No energy was spared. Nothing was wasted. Everything was taken into perfect account.

All tears have been wiped away; there is no more death, neither sorrow, nor crying, nor pain, for all those things had passed away.

Somewhere, in an isolated, barely thought of corner of the system, a creature walks the rows of corn one by one, watches a flower bloom, and listens to the wilderness.

A Catalogue for the End of Humanity

First published in *Orion's Belt*

Emmeline was allowed to pick from three 'archetype' versions of herself, much like how she might have chosen a home droid from a catalogue. The ones best representing her were projected up onto the platform—her whole life and fears and experiences filtered down to ones and zeroes, color-coded and bullet-pointed with all the best features of each. She wondered how they'd calculated something like that.

The first version of her was skipping, the kind of thing she'd only done before the wars, before the Cold. Back then, she didn't care if other people thought it was childish. Her curls and smile betrayed her naivete—hardships were losing friends and failing classes. That version also encompassed a simple joy Emmeline envied. Before her first love with all the hope of finding her.

Everything was so much brighter back then, even the colours, as if someone had turned up the saturation to unnatural levels, but the years, or time, or her outlook had blunted the blues and greens and mixed them in with grey.

'Do I lose it all? Everything that's not in these files?' she asked Dr Orlean.

The freckled woman clearly hated the question and pushed up her glasses with a grimace that briefly hardened the crow's feet by her eyes. Maybe she had answered it too many times or was afraid the answer might push people away.

'Yes,' she admitted, 'but that's the upload price. The system hasn't been perfected yet—we haven't had the time. Meaning we can only store archetypes. Imperfect copies.'

'But it'll still be me.'

Dr Orlean jabbed a few buttons on the monitor. Emmeline's first version halted and dug through her bag, the one she'd made herself and covered in pins. It had burned along with everything else. Her archetype pulled out a camera to snap a few shots of a crow that had landed nearby.

'God, I still have that camera, you know? I thought I'd pawn it away for food. I haven't photographed anything since…'

'You, yes?' Dr Orlean asked.

Emmeline nodded, first loosely, then firmly.

Her second version was clad in frontline armour, boots deep in the mud that she remembered felt like quicksand. Her cloak spoke to the Cold, and the fresh wound on her forehead spoke of how close she'd come to death. The Indestructible Orbital Fortifications had fallen—'Unsinkable too, I reckon,' she'd said at the time. Her people were fleeing, and *they* were coming.

The Cold wasn't something around her; it was a part of her, bleeding into her fingers and eyes and drawing out the last gasps of life she had in her lungs. She desperately fought to kindle a fire, but the flames gave up over and over and over—till she did, too.

The cliff face. A fall. Darkness.

Emmeline didn't know who had saved her.

Nothing had changed her more than those days in the Cold, and amongst the terror and pain and scars, she had also come to know herself better. She missed the days when taking a good photo of a crow was her only concern, but there was more to her now. More meat. More thought. More cynicism. She had saved people and been saved and felt the pain that reminded her to live. Emmeline marvelled at how the projection captured it all in the depths of her eyes, or maybe it was a Rorschach test, and she was seeing what she needed to.

It was hell, but she couldn't crawl through hell and pretend she hadn't.

'I wish I could take some parts and leave others behind. Pick and choose.'

'Afraid that's not possible. We tried storing fully digitized constructs, lifetime memories and all, and mixed constructs, but they fractured. It likes whole, completed consciousnesses with a specific environmental backdrop. Narratives it can organize everything into.'

Emmeline pursed her lips, understanding. 'But people change.'

'Exactly, but for the moment, it doesn't understand that.'

There was a cruel irony to it. The universe had moulded her into a different person time and again, and now it was making her choose which would be the real Emmeline.

The third version of her was like looking into a warped mirror: it was her, but with something uncanny and bent out of shape. Maybe she didn't recognize herself or didn't want to and still imagined herself as young and beautiful, or middle-aged and grizzled. The wound from the second version had healed into a crescent, motley scar. Her one good eye sagged with memory, searching for someone that could look back at her. Not with a naïve, ignorant love like in the first projection, but one that understood her.

All of her.

She had found someone like that in Milanka. They met in the decrepit ruins of Koper during the worst of it. A fight for the last scraps of food. Milanka won but shared the stale loaf of bread and half a mouldy potato with her, anyway. They'd travelled together for years and wouldn't have made it half as far without the other. They'd made a life, or what life they could, and lived it together till Milanka couldn't anymore, and Emmeline endured the remnants of what was left.

If the Cold was the curse of her second life, loneliness was the curse of her third.

It was a deeper, more wretched kind of pain, and one, in her private thoughts, she sometimes wished she could live without.

'How long do I have?'

Dr Orlean didn't check her watch. 'They're coming.'

'Uh-huh.' She stepped back from the three versions.

'You were picked for several reasons, but this might be the only thing that survives out in the cosmos.'

'Half-baked digits of a handful of us?' She could only scoff.

'We tried our best.'

'I'm sorry.'

Dr Orlean waved her off. 'I'll prep the digitization chamber, and if you'd like, you can decide privately. It is, after all, a medical decision. We sometimes forget that.'

Emmeline gave her thanks and was left alone in the small, industrial room. No time for the usual beautification of a place like that.

It would be so nice to return to a simple, gentle life, but she couldn't forget the Cold or the loneliness. Or perhaps she could. She had been many people across her life, but she could have been a thousand other people too—if not for the wars, if not for others, if the cards had dealt her a kinder hand.

'It might be good to try again.' Her voice curved with childish inquisitiveness.

With a heavy finger, she chose the new life she would return to.